In Your Orbit

In Your Orbit contains content readers may find triggering, as it explores anxiety, depression and suicidal thoughts. The book also contains references to rape, alcoholism and school shootings.

LITTLE TIGER
An imprint of Little Tiger Press Limited
1 Coda Studios, 189 Munster Road,
London SW6 6AW

Imported into the EEA by Penguin Random House Ireland,
Morrison Chambers, 32 Nassau Street, Dublin D02 YH68

www.littletiger.co.uk

First published in Denmark by Gyldendal as 'Kvantespring' 2020
This edition first published in Great Britain 2023

ISBN: 978-1-78895-604-8

A CIP catalogue record for this book is available from the British Library.

Supported by the Danish Arts Foundation
Published by agreement with Salomonsson Agency

Printed and bound in the UK.

The Forest Stewardship Council® (FSC®) is a global, not-for-profit organization dedicated to the promotion of responsible forest management worldwide. FSC defines standards based on agreed principles for responsible forest stewardship that are supported by environmental, social, and economic stakeholders. To learn more, visit www.fsc.org

10 9 8 7 6 5 4 3 2 1

Lise Villadsen

Translated by Caroline Waight

LITTLE TIGER
LONDON

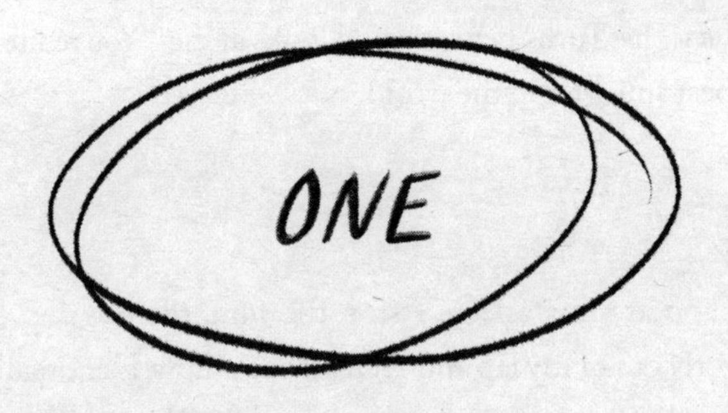

She's lying with her head in my lap and I can smell her freshly washed hair, but I can feel how messy it is too. The bird's nests in my sister's mid-length hair remind me of my own, the ones I tear at with a comb each morning.

There's a laptop on the bed in front of us, the screen flickering with voices and light. I lift my eyes and glance towards the half-open window. The sound of nearing summer drifts inside. Blackbirds whistling, the drone of a lawnmower in a garden far away.

"Don't stop," says Cecilie.

"I'm not stopping."

"You're thinking about something else. I can tell."

"Not really." Then my fingers set to work again. I stroke the soft skin at her temples, moving behind her ear, down her neck.

She sighs. Turns her head and looks at me. "You're literally the best snuggler in the world."

As soon as she's asleep, I stop the film, see-saw her head gingerly out of my lap and set it on the pillow. Her breathing is already heavy. There's a calm about her that's never there when she's awake.

Jonas has texted, asking if I'm up for ice cream at the harbour tomorrow once we're done with class, so we can start planning for when we go interrailing. I tell him sure. Then I ask what he's doing.

Got dragged to this crappy minigolf place. Kicking Oliver's arse!

He sends me a picture of himself – it must have been taken by his older brother – in which he's got a club balanced across the back of his neck and shoulders and his arms resting over the shaft. It might actually have looked macho if it wasn't for the yellow bucket hat perched on his head and the cheesy grin plastered across his sunburnt face.

What are you up to?

Movie. Killing time.

Go get some sun, sourpuss.

And look like you? LOL

Sunscreen gives you spots is his parting shot.

"Did you finish watching your film?" asks Mum when I walk into the kitchen. She's peeling potatoes over the sink. Her hands move swiftly and efficiently, her eyes fixed on what she's doing.

I start to lay the table. "No, she fell asleep."

"Ah, that's good. She can squeeze in half an hour before we eat."

I put four plates on the table. Four glasses. Each time I pass the open living-room door, I look at Dad, who's sitting with his legs crossed on the sofa, his computer on his lap. He's balancing it on one knee. The TV's on.

"Mum? I was thinking. Maybe we should do something nice next weekend. The four of us? Before the revision period gets under way."

"Absolutely," she says. "Good idea."

"Maybe we could play croquet." I take the cutlery out of the drawer. "And have a barbecue."

"That sounds nice," says Mum. But she stops peeling. She's silent a moment before adding, "Do you think Cecilie will enjoy it, if we can just get the ball rolling?"

"Yeah. That's what I was thinking."

"OK then, let's do that. Maybe you can find the croquet stuff and set it up on Saturday."

"Sure."

She puffs the hair away from her forehead and smiles. "Come here."

I go to her and she lays a wet hand on my shoulder. There's a scent of earth and raw potato.

"Thank you," she says.

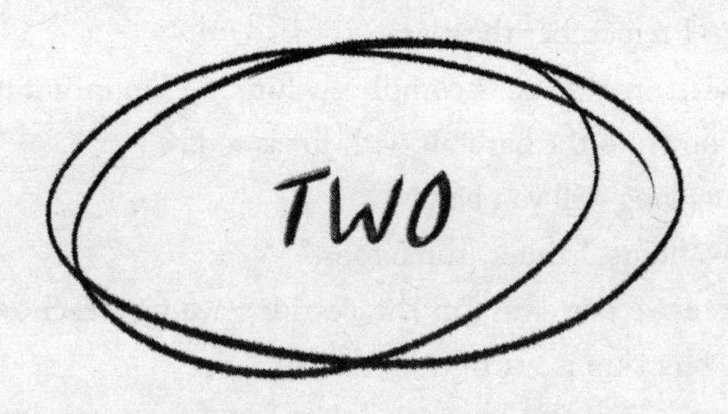

My sister's moving extra slowly today. The motion of her legs round and round is constant, unfluctuating, no shift in speed, whether we're cycling along the flat forest track or up the hill past the shopping centre. I match my pace to hers. When cars come past, I trundle in behind her. She's hunched, her back curved. It's something to do with how badly she's sleeping right now. Her spine doesn't want to straighten when she wakes.

"Can we go home together? Later?" she asks as we put our bikes in the rack outside the big red-brick buildings.

"I get out at three."

"Me too," she says and looks relieved.

Right now, my sister needs me more than usual. Sometimes it's like I can feel her better than I can feel myself. As though her body is a magnet, pulling me in.

Then I remember the plan.

"Wait, sorry," I say. "I completely forgot – I'm meant to be going down to the harbour with Jonas today."

"How long will you be?"

"Two hours, I think. Three tops."

When we part ways in the corridor, we give each other a hug. Her skin is warm from the sun.

"See you, Eelie," I say.

"See you, Shrimp."

When I was little and wanted to say 'Cecilie', it always came out like 'Eelia', and for some reason the 'a' disappeared when our parents pointed it out and I tried to pronounce the name correctly. Then she started calling me Shrimp and suddenly our parents had two types of seafood as daughters.

She walks off towards the third years' corridor, where the graduating class's rooms are located. She's moving slowly, same as she did on the bike. Kind of like a sleepwalker.

I wait until she's out of sight before I head towards 1.Z's classroom.

Jonas is already in our usual spot: at the back, far away from the door.

"You look like you spent the weekend in a freaking church," he says, darting a glance at my pale arms.

Ignoring him, I put my laptop on the table next to my bottle of water.

"You'll start rotting if you don't get enough vitamin D, you know. Your bones'll snap if you so much as squeak out a fart."

"Are you really that worried about my vitamin D levels?" I say. "I'm off to Crete for, like, a week in August."

"Um, hello. Doesn't our trip count?"

"You mean that crappy little backpacking thing?"

Jonas swats me.

Veronica turns to us from the desk in front. "Remember there's a meeting at lunchtime about decorating the trucks."

"OK, where?" I ask.

"Just in the cafeteria. But you've got to be there."

She taps her index finger against the side of her small round nose, smiling so broadly that her glasses joggle.

Ever since Veronica joined our class before Christmas, Jonas has been saying she's got a certain vibe. "She's even freakier than I am," he likes to say, with admiration in his eyes. "You can tell just by looking at her."

I was the one who came up with the name Veronicaraptor. Not that she looks like a dinosaur, but she still reminds me of one, clattering down the hallway in her purple Crocs, sinking her claws into the first person she can catch.

"I'll be there," I say, forcing myself to smile back.

"That means you too, Jonas." Veronica points at him before she turns back round.

"Of course, honey," Jonas whispers to me, staring at all the curls down the back of Veronica's neck.

I slap at him. "Try and act a little bit normal, OK?"

"It's hard."

It really *is* hard for my best friend, I think. When I met

him on the first day of school nine months ago, he was standing in the middle of the cafeteria in Hawaiian-print Bermuda shorts and the tatty yellow bucket hat he wears all year round because it was his dad's. *Are you seriously worried about the lack of diversity in this place too*? were his first words to me, but even before he'd opened his mouth I could tell he was a one-off.

At lunchtime, we go downstairs and sit at the Z table in the Bathtub, as we've dubbed our cafeteria because it's a big, cold, rectangular hall located directly underneath the open space on the first floor, where the third years eat. Every now and then, we get spattered with food or drink. That's why we call their cafeteria 'the Sink'. The first week they squirted remoulade, hitting Jonas smack in the neck with a thick stream. He says the feeling of lumpy pickle dripping down your vertebrae is unforgettable.

"Can everybody hear me?" Veronica is sitting cross-legged on the table.

If there's one thing about Veronica that makes you feel kind of bad for her, it's her desperate need to make people like her by taking on the jobs they can't be arsed to do: collecting money, clearing up after homework club, all that idiotic stuff. Now she's fussing about the first years decorating the third years' student trucks, the ones they'll drive around in all day after graduation. It's more than a month away, but of course she's already chomping at the bit.

"We're meeting at half eight right outside by the trucks," she says, her voice loud and clear. "Everybody transfer fifteen kroner to me by the twentieth at the latest, then I'll sort out the balloons and bunting. Some of us can go and get beech leaves when we meet up. Someone else can grab breakfast. And if we can all bring a couple of bin bags to put the leaves in, that would be awesome."

"Can't you also just buy the bin bags and the breakfast?" says Isak, rocking backwards on his chair as he yawns. "Isn't it, like, a hundred times easier if there's one person in charge of everything?"

Veronica's cheeks turn pink.

"Does she look like your mummy?" asks Jonas, which makes Isak mutter something inaudible.

My phone buzzes in my pocket. I check the message under the table.

I need you.

I nudge Jonas, whisper, "Back in a minute," then head out of the Bathtub and down the corridor to the girls' loos. That's always where she texts from. I shut the door behind me. Of the three stalls, only one is bolted red.

I knock gently. "Eelie? It's me."

She answers. Lets me in. Then she shuts the door behind us, locks it and slumps on to the closed toilet seat.

"I can't be here." She's gazing up at me with wide, already damp eyes.

There's a knot in my stomach that will never loosen. It just lives down there, ever since it moved in a few years ago. Now it tightens.

"You want me to take you home?" I crouch down in front of her, holding her hand. It feels limp in mine. "Can you get out of class?"

Even back when she was in first year, Cecilie got a written warning about her absences and they called her in for a meeting with our parents. Since then, there's been a degree of understanding on the teachers' side about deadlines for assignments but not about missing class. Mum and Cecilie talk every day about her absence rate, as though it was the weather forecast. They calculate and recalculate how often she can play truant, precisely how many physics and Danish and PE classes she's able to skip before the penalty kicks in: the school won't count any of her marks throughout the year, so she'll have to take final exams in everything.

"I … can't … can't … breathe." Cecilie is exhaling jerkily.

"Do you want me to call Mum?"

"Don't … know."

"OK. Would you rather—"

She puts a knuckle in her mouth. I can almost see her running through the whole list in her head, like she once told me she did: *Don't throw up, don't faint, don't make a scene.*

"Take some deep breaths," I say, removing her finger from her mouth. "I'll ring Mum."

She gasps twice, then starts breathing normally. Now she's just sitting immobile on the toilet seat, staring into space while I grab my phone and make the call.

"Astrid, hi. Is Cecilie OK?" Our mother's radar is fine-tuned. She can pick up bad weather even at a distance.

"She's not doing so great."

"Can you calm her down?"

I glance sidelong at my sister. "I don't think so."

"Try and get her to take some of those really deep breaths. Could you go for a little walk before the next lesson starts?"

Cecilie begins to sob in earnest.

"Mum, I think you should come and get her."

I can hear my mother starting to pack up her things, clattering coffee cups and rustling papers in one long unbroken move towards the door.

"OK, I'm on my way. Just wait in the car park."

I hang up and crouch back down in front of Cecilie. Taking her hand, I give it a squeeze. "Mum's coming. Are your things still in the classroom?"

She nods. Wipes her cheek.

"OK, I'll go and get them. Be back in a minute. Then we'll wait for Mum together."

The 3.Z classroom is empty. Everybody's in the Sink and most of them have taken their bags. Cecilie's things are slumped against the wall: her backpack, her worn denim jacket. As though she couldn't even manage to find a seat.

As I gather her belongings, I wonder how long she's been sitting in that toilet stall. If she got no further than dumping her stuff at eight in the morning before it all got too much. Sometimes she can get it under control, she says, if she does her breathing exercises. But it's past twelve now.

On the way out of the door, I nearly bump into two of my sister's classmates. One is Fillip, a red-haired guy with an eyebrow piercing, who I'm pretty sure has no idea I'm Cecilie's sister.

The other is someone I actually know.

Kristoffer Boldsen.

"Your ex-neighbour," as Jonas dubbed him after I told him about that weird pocket of time seven years ago when he, Cecilie and I lived next door to each other and played together, before he moved to Nuuk. I always thought he looked striking, with the black hair he inherited from his Greenlandic dad and the dark blue eyes he got from his mum. It's just annoying how obviously he knows it.

"Whoa," he says, stepping aside so we just miss bumping into each other in the doorway. And then my name, like a small extra surprise: "Astrid?"

I've still not got used to how deep and different his voice has become. It's been a year since he moved back to Denmark with his mum, after his parents' divorce, and he always says hi when we pass each other in the hall. It's like he thinks he owes me the attention because he left so suddenly all those years ago.

"Hey," I reply.

I'm not dumb. I can see Fillip nudging Kristoffer because he's acknowledging a person with boobs.

"What were you doing in there?" Kristoffer looks at the bag and jacket in my hands. He smiles. "Stealing, eh?"

"What's it got to do with you?"

"Erm," says Fillip, raising the pierced eyebrow, before I slip past them and out of the door. "You let her talk to you that way? Really?"

I stride swiftly back to the loos and find Cecilie. Taking her arm, I guide her past the cafeteria and out into the sunshine, into the car park.

"Gulls are psychopaths," I say as we stand there and wait, looking up at the sky.

The white-and-grey birds are circling above the cars, as though they've caught sight of a dead fish among them.

"Have you ever stared into a gull's eyes? Totally dead. Apparently, they're also the least faithful birds in the world."

I shoot her a glance. She's totally white in the face.

"Is it better if I don't talk?" I ask. "Shall we sit down instead?"

"Just stand," she says. "Quietly."

"OK," I say and hold her hand.

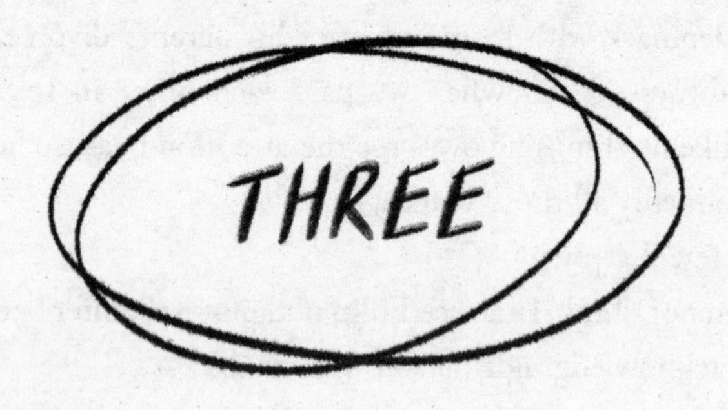

The meeting is over by the time I get back to the Bathtub. Jonas is chatting with Veronica, gnawing on a sandwich, so I have to prod his shoulder and tell him we need to talk.

We retreat a couple of metres to the coffee machine.

"I've got to cancel our hang later."

"What?! But we were going to plan our trip today!"

"Sorry. I know." I get a coffee with milk and offer Jonas one too, but he says he needs to get back to his sandwich asap. He looks pissed off, almost offended.

"It's – look, Cecilie's doing really badly. I had to call our mum – she just came and picked her up."

"What's wrong with her?" he asks, although he knows perfectly well.

"The same thing that's always wrong," I say. I don't feel like going into details.

"Didn't she get over it?"

"You don't just 'get over' anxiety," I say.

"But wasn't it getting better?"

Jonas is right. When I met him last summer, my sister was going through a decent patch. Winter, on the other hand, was bad. First there were the marks she got at the end of November, which gave her a meltdown because she'd slipped down a grade in four subjects. Then there was her coursework, which she only managed to hand in because Mum sat with her in front of the computer every evening. Mostly she just switched off when she came home from school, her expression a blank screen, hibernating, doing nothing but lying in her room and sleeping and sleeping and asking for crispbread sandwiches. When spring came, everything lightened a bit. And now here we are again.

"Yeah," I say. "It got better. But it isn't any more."

Jonas starts picking at his nail. "Can't she just be with your mum today?"

"It'll be a more normal atmosphere if it's the three of us."

"Explain it to me," he says, getting that pissed-off look again that doesn't suit the cheery yellow of his bucket hat.

I take a quick sip of coffee, burning my tongue. "When our mum takes time off work and it's just the two of them sitting at home, it gets really … like somebody's sick. It's unnatural. It feels more normal and everyday if I'm there too."

I can tell Jonas doesn't understand. That part of him

doesn't want to understand.

"We can do it on Thursday?" I say.

"What if she's anxious on Thursday too?"

"Look, be fair," I say.

"OK. Thursday then."

His eyes wander back towards the Bathtub. I'm sure he's looking for Veronica.

"I think it's because of exams. They're starting soon," I say because I really want Jonas to understand this. "She's also sleeping really badly."

"But you can get help for anxiety about exams," he says. "Can't her doctor give her some beta blockers?"

"You can't just give someone beta blockers all the time. It doesn't solve anything."

"What about some proper medication then?"

"It's not that simple."

"Yeah, well," he says, "I'm gonna flip out soon if I don't get down to the harbour for an ice cream and a bit of psychoanalysis with my favourite therapist."

All autumn Jonas was having a serious crisis because he 'semi' fell in love with Stephanie from 1.B, who ended up getting blackout drunk at the school ball and lurched around, telling everybody she was sure he was into guys. January and February were better because he got a hug and a declaration that she wanted to be friends, which he found really encouraging until he discovered she'd already secretly started dating Isak back in November.

"I thought we'd sorted most of your stuff out?" I say. "Didn't we agree you should focus solely on yourself until after the summer holidays?"

He scowls at me. "You want me to find another therapist?"

"Threats aren't very nice."

"Just saying."

When I get home, Cecilie is worse.

She's lying in bed with the duvet wrapped tightly round her. Her eyes are closed. She's got her old, dingy stuffed elephant clamped against her chin. Her breathing is heavy, but every so often a violent spasm runs through her body. I stare at her for a while. My eyes wander to the poster above her bed, which I gave her as a birthday present so many years ago that Mum was the one who actually bought it. By now, all the edges are tattered. Winnie-the-Pooh and Piglet are holding hands and underneath, in funny, lopsided letters, it says:

You are braver than you believe,
Stronger than you seem,
And smarter than you think.

I walk into the kitchen to find Mum.

"We'll just let her sleep. She's so tired all the time."

"Her back hurts too," I say.

"Yes, I know."

Mum takes off her reading glasses and rubs her eyes. She's got her laptop open and a mass of papers spread out across the table, where there's also a bottle of vitamin pills and a dirty yoghurt bowl from this morning. My mother often brings her work home from the office because of Cecilie. It's been happening almost as long as I can remember.

"We're taking her to Bruuns Clinic next week for a chat," says Mum. "New psychologist."

"Isn't Kirsten there any more?"

"Yeah, but they reached a bit of a deadlock last winter, remember?"

'Deadlock' is code for the fact that Cecilie convinced our parents she was going to take the train alone, until Kirsten rang after the second appointment and asked Mum if there'd been a misunderstanding and they didn't want to pay for the sessions after all, because no one had turned up.

"I spoke to someone called Nanna instead. She's young. That might be better." She delves back into her paperwork, but it's only a few seconds before she looks up again. "Would you mind helping Cecilie get ready to leave for her appointment?"

"Sure," I say. "Of course."

"We need to be there at four on Monday." She runs a hand through her hair. "And now I just have to do a couple of things here before I die of stress."

I sit down in the living room with a book. I read for a bit, trying not to wonder whether Jonas decided to invite Veronica to the harbour instead. I picture a bird's-eye view, the purple Crocs and the yellow bucket hat moving among ice-cream kiosks and sailing boats.

After an hour and a half, Cecilie calls.

I go into her room. Mum comes running from the kitchen and reaches the edge of the bed first. She sits down, stroking my sister's hair.

"Are you feeling better, sweetheart?"

"A bit."

My sister is doubled up like a kicked hedgehog under the duvet. I ask if there's anything she'd like to do. We keep watching the film we started yesterday, which we've seen at least ten times before. I scratch her scalp, but she falls asleep again after only twenty minutes. And when it comes to dinnertime, she doesn't want to sit up at the table. Our mother simply puts a plate of rice and curried meatballs on her desk in case she feels like some.

While I eat with my parents, Mum's knife and fork spend ninety per cent of the time on the edge of her plate. She keeps turning her glass of water round and round on the table, although she doesn't drink it, and shooting the occasional glance across to the other side of the table where my father is stuffing himself.

"I had to pick up Cecilie from school today," she says at last. Her voice is muted, although the door is shut. "She was absolutely beside herself. Crying and shaking when we got home."

"What happened?" asks Dad as though there's a logical answer to that question.

Mum looks at me.

"She texted me," I say. "From the toilets," I add, with a mouthful of food.

"She's sleeping very badly at the moment," continues Mum. "She's been complaining about back pain again and says she can't breathe when she wakes up. I think we should book an appointment with the doctor. Get him to listen to her lungs and reassure her."

"There's nothing wrong with her lungs," says Dad.

"We need to take it seriously when she says she's in pain."

"It's our job to tell her there's nothing physically wrong with her. We can't take up the doctor's time with that."

"It's the pressure of exams," Mum says as though she hasn't heard him. "It's going to be tough. I don't know how we're going to get her through it..."

Dad puts a meatball into his mouth, chewing quickly. "Wasn't there something about a new psychologist?"

"Yes," says Mum. "The first session's on Monday."

He nods to himself a few times, as though that ought to be answer enough to the question of what to do about Cecilie. Then he says, "And why are you letting her lie in there now?"

"She's tired."

"This isn't helping her."

"What do you mean?"

"It's important for us to set some ground rules," he says. "We eat dinner in here. Together. As a family. It's no good treating her like a stubborn three-year-old."

"All right then, you go in there and force her." Mum puts the glass of water to her lips and swallows a few quick mouthfuls. "Yes, I think you should do that."

Dad gives her a long stare, the kind he uses to build a wall. Then he keeps on eating.

I saw a documentary series once about children with cancer. Their parents were going through an enormous crisis and they were enormously present. They held their children. Kissed them and reassured them that everything would be fine. Everybody in the families cried and hugged when there was bad news, and it really was horrible, but somehow I couldn't help feeling they had something we didn't.

Maybe it would be easier for my parents if my sister was lying in a hospital bed with tubes coming out of her nose.

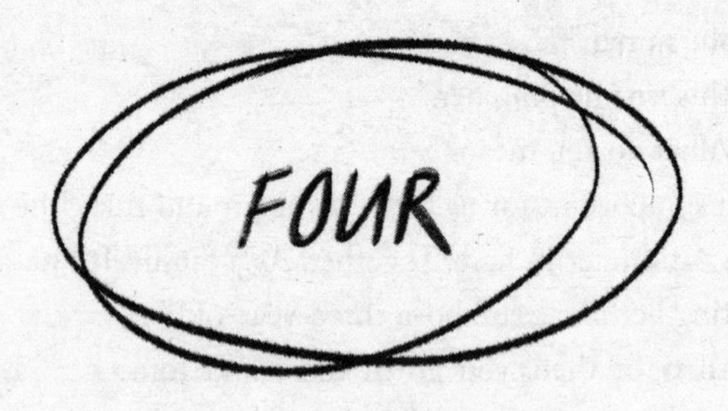

"Move your bum so there's room for everybody!" She elbows Jonas, making him shift along the bench, and suddenly I'm not sitting opposite my best friend, but opposite Veronicaraptor. She opens a pink lunchbox and takes out a sandwich. Two pieces of seeded rye bread around a slice of cheese that looks sweaty and smells like an old gym mat even at this distance.

"So, what subjects do you think we're getting tested on this term?" she asks, taking a sizeable bite of the sandwich.

A completely idiotic question. Like it's remotely interesting to know what we think we're getting when it won't be announced till Monday.

"I've got a nasty feeling about social studies," says Jonas.

"Me too!"

Of course she does.

"What about you, Astrid?" she asks after finishing her mouthful. "What are you most nervous about getting?"

"I don't care."

"Really?" she says.

"Astrid always plays it so cool," says Jonas. "But she sucks at biology."

I'm about to snap back when suddenly they're both goggling at something behind me, over my head. I turn and look up.

It's Kristoffer. He's standing very close, in a way normal people just don't do.

"What have you done with Cecilie?" he asks, looking down at me with a face like I might have hidden her under the table between my legs.

It's not just Veronica and Jonas staring now, it's the entire 1.Z table.

"She's not well," I say.

I don't know how much he's noticed since he came back to Denmark and joined her class. If he's got any concept of what my sister's fighting, or whether he just assumes her absences are down to skiving, colds, weakness.

"She's not texting me back," he says.

"I'll tell her."

The corner of his mouth twitches slightly upward, slightly down, as though he's struggling over whether or not to smile. "You don't need to tell her she's not texting me back. I'm pretty sure she already knows."

One of them, Jonas or Veronica, stifles a giggle.

"It's not important," he continues. "Well, actually it is."

I don't know how someone can change their mind so quickly.

"She promised I could borrow a water blaster before Friday."

The last day of school makes sense when you're fifteen and you're allowed to smother cheeky twelve-year-olds in shaving foam. But this is a bunch of people who are supposed to be acting like they're nearly grown-ups, and on Friday they're planning to spray us with an indeterminate fluid probably consisting of equal parts piss, water and oil.

"I can just bring it tomorrow," I say. "If you want."

"Nah." He pulls a face. "I'm not interested in lugging that big neon-green motherfucker around all day. Can't I just come by tonight and pick it up?"

It's already running through my head like a movie: the moment when I tell Cecilie that Kristoffer is going to show up at our house, standing at our front door, his voice, presence, questions.

I say again, "I can just bring it over to yours."

"Yeah, you can do that." He takes a few steps backwards, smiling. "We can have a quick water fight."

"Oh, you bet."

His smile widens. "Do you remember all those times you went running around naked in my garden, screaming while I blasted you?"

I just stare at him, ice-cold, and thankfully he goes. Not until I turn back to Jonas and Veronica do my cheeks begin to burn.

"He did not just say that," says Jonas.

Veronica is looking way too interested in me.

"I knew him when I was little," I say, meeting her eyes. "And FYI, he was always the one who ended up the wettest."

"Yeah, back then!" says Jonas, laughing.

I take a big sip from my water bottle. "He's an idiot."

"Whose house you're going over to this evening," adds Veronica.

It occurs to me that I don't even know where Kristoffer lives.

I put my bike in the garden shed and start searching for the water blaster. It's at the very back, in the darkest corner, on top of a stack of old wooden boards I think my dad was planning to make into a deckchair several summers ago. But he didn't have enough of what my dad never has enough of in his life – time.

The water blaster is entwined in cobwebs and covered with dark blotches of mould. I take it into the utility room and wipe it down with a damp cloth until it looks like its old neon-green self. It's the larger model, holding nearly two litres of water.

We used to have two, but mine broke years ago when I lost my temper over something I've since forgotten and flung it on to the ground, shattering the plastic water tank. Last year I was allowed to borrow Cecilie's for the final day of middle school. Now Kristoffer's allowed. That must mean my sister's already decided she's not coming on Friday. It's traditional for the third years to dress up in something silly, colourful or naughty, but my sister hasn't said a word about what she's going to wear; she's not gone sniffing round my wardrobe or Mum's for a colourful piece of old clothing she can cut up.

I half fill the gun with water and try it on the wall of the house. It shoots a thick, consistent stream every time I pump.

As I walk inside, I hear voices coming from my sister's room. Mum's not home from work today and since the driveway's still empty that must mean Caroline has come to visit.

They're sitting with the door open, each cupping a mug of tea with both hands.

"Hi, Eelie," I say. "Hi, Caro."

"Hi, Astrid." Caroline's nostrils quiver slightly as she shoots me a rapid smile.

I've always thought of my sister's friend as a rumpled, frightened squirrel: red hair, vigilant eyes. Caroline is what my mum calls a 'good girl', and she certainly is – there's no better girl than Caroline on *earth*, that's for sure, but mostly I think Cecilie would never have befriended such a dreary person if she was in her right mind.

Ever since I first met Caroline, I've felt like she isn't genuinely interested in my sister. She just hangs out with Cecilie every once in a while, maybe because she doesn't have anyone else. It might sound harsh but she's always struck me as kind of blah, and even though she's not the worst, she's definitely not what I want for my sister. Cecilie deserves a true friend, someone who can make her laugh.

"I just wanted to drop by and bring round some notes we got today," says Caroline, half rising, as if to leave just because I showed up.

"I'm heading out again," I say quickly.

Caroline sinks back on to the bed.

"OK?" Cecilie darts me one of her good smiles. One of the lively ones. As though she's teasing me a little. As though she wants to say, *What are you up to now, Shrimp?*

"I'll be back soon."

A quick search on the school intranet tells me Kristoffer has moved into a development on the other side of town. I decide to take the long way there: first a slow spin through the harbour while the afternoon sun warms my bare arms, then past the dog park, where I stop for a minute and watch the dogs, freed from their leashes, hurtling across the grass, their tongues lolling out of their mouths or exploring each other's backsides.

When we were little, Cecilie and I were always bugging our parents to get a dog. Our dad didn't like the idea of hair on the sofa, and anyway he has some sort of allergy to fur, so nothing ever came of it. But occasionally I wonder whether a dog might have changed things. I read once that an animal's affection can cure all kinds of things: loneliness, depression, anxiety. It's funny, really, that human love doesn't have the same power.

When I reach the labyrinth of small, identical brick houses, I cycle up and down the road for a while, passing number thirty-six a couple of times before I come to a halt. My bike doesn't have a kickstand, so I just push it up against the hedge and lock it out of habit, then tuck the water blaster under my arm and walk up the garden path. My finger hasn't so much as touched the bell before the door is flung open in a single movement.

I can't help looking him up and down. Grey granddad slippers, joggers, a T-shirt with wet splotches on the front and a chequered tea towel slung over his shoulder. His fingers are dripping with soapy water and the smell of washing-up liquid reminds me of the time when we blew soap bubbles together out on the street.

"Hey," he says. "I thought you were coming tonight?"

"Tonight?"

"Isn't that what we agreed?"

He whisks the tea towel off his shoulder and dries his hands before flipping it back into place.

"I don't think we agreed anything."

"OK, well, I'm doing the dishes right now," he says as though that would interest me.

I hold out the water blaster. "Here you go."

He takes it.

"Who is it?" shouts his mother from inside the house. I recognize her voice straight away.

"Nobody!" Kristoffer yells back, which somehow really offends me. He steps outside and shuts the door behind him.

"Is Cecilie feeling better? Is she coming to school tomorrow?"

I pretend to give it some actual thought while I take a slight step backwards. "I think so."

"She's gotta be in good nick for Friday," he says. "You only graduate once."

I say, "But you're not graduating on Friday."

"It's the first part of the process. It's the kick-off." He rattles through the list. "Last day of school, exams, graduation day, the truck, the parties." He adds, "Plus the marathon boozing."

"You can always skip a few steps," I say.

"Can you?"

He's leaning casually against the door. I can't help staring at his hands, the way they're holding the water blaster. Not hard, not forcefully, but almost softly, as though he's cradling a baby against his body. When I look up and meet his eyes, he's staring at me like it's super obvious I was gawping.

"OK, well, see you." I hurry back to my bike. As I'm bending over the saddle to grab the lock, I'm hit in the back of the neck by a thick stream of water.

"Hey!" I whirl back round.

Slowly Kristoffer lowers the weapon, smiling. Such a dumb, boyish smile, like he's twelve years old.

"Just wanted to check you were awake."

"I *am* awake!"

He keeps smiling. Then he shoots another jet in my direction. This time I manage to sidestep it so the water only hits the tip of my elbow.

"Stop it!"

"Stop being so touchy," he says. "It's *water*!"

I can feel heat pressing behind my eyes, which is completely stupid. He's just rude and idiotic and doesn't get that things have changed, that neither of us is a kid any more.

Quickly wrenching open the lock, I drag my bike out of the hedge.

"Hey ... Astrid..."

Before he can say another word, I've jumped on the saddle and set off.

I'm home at half five the next day. Cecilie cycled back from school alone and Jonas and I spent the afternoon planning our trip. We've included Germany and Hungary, Berlin and Budapest. When I step through the door, the kitchen is empty. I follow the voices.

"I'm just afraid you'll regret it, sweetheart. That's the only reason I'm saying this."

"I've got to study."

"But the subjects won't be announced till Monday. You don't know what exams you're supposed to be studying for."

I stop in the doorway of Cecilie's room. "What are you talking about?"

"The last day of school," says Mum.

They both look at me for a brief moment, then fix their eyes back on each other.

"Can't we just drop it?"

"What about just going to part of the day? Maybe you could—" Mum puts her hand on Cecilie's shoulder but she immediately shoves it off, sending the hand flying through the air before it lands back in Mum's lap.

"Do you need to interfere in *everything*?!"

Mum takes a deep, patient breath. "I can see you don't feel up to this right now. That's OK. We can talk about it later."

"I don't *want* to talk about it later." Cecilie's eyelids are trembling a fraction – it's a tic she's had for as long as I can remember.

"No, sorry," says Mum. "Then we won't say any more about it."

"I just really don't *feel* like it," Cecilie says, opening her eyes wide again. "I mean I really, really *don't*."

"OK, then you won't go." Mum sounds tired but also relieved. Like she's retreating from a battle she knew in advance she'd lose. Now, cautiously, she strokes Cecilie's hand, and this time she's allowed. "The whole point is that it's a fun day."

"It just won't be for me. At all."

"I can see that."

"And I'm so tired. Being in class is so insanely hard. My back kills me when I sit on those chairs. It's like torture!"

"All right. Now you just rest, sweetheart."

Mum goes out into the garden. We can hear her through the open window, moving the furniture around. Maybe she's sat down for a cup of coffee. Or maybe she's just staring into space. That's a sense I get more and more often: that our mother is walking around, snapping inside, like a twig stepped on by accident.

I stay with Cecilie. We put on a film. She nestles close to me. Her legs are warm and bare and she rubs them against mine.

"Did you have a nice time with Jonas?" she asks when we're ten minutes into the film. I thought she was asleep.

"Mm."

"Do you think your trip will happen?"

"Well, we've already bought our interrail passes."

"So you're off in July?"

"It's only for two weeks. But..." I'm about to say, *I think it will be fun*. "Maybe we won't be able to do it right. Maybe we'll board the wrong train and get off in Russia and be bunged in prison because Jonas says something stupid about Putin."

She doesn't laugh. She doubles up under the duvet as though somebody's kicked her in the stomach. "I really hate myself."

"Don't say stuff like that."

"Yeah, well, I can't do anything right, can I?"

My brain struggles to find something to say. She used to be good at baking and handstands, but she hasn't baked since her birthday two years ago, and she's been complaining for ages that it hurts to move.

"You're good at physics," I say. "And maths."

She rolls her eyes. "I just feel like Mum and Dad are massively disappointed in me."

"They're not."

"And I hate it when Mum tells me I'm going to regret something. I really hate it! Like I have a real choice."

"You've started saying 'real' a lot."

She uncurls slightly, smiling. "It's a good word."

"Kristoffer borrowed your water blaster, by the way." I should have told her yesterday, but for some reason I needed a bit of a run-up to spit it out.

"Oh fuck," she says. "I forgot I promised. When did you talk to him? Was he pissed off?"

"Why would he be pissed off? Didn't you see him today?"

"We never talk in class," she says, like it's the most natural thing in the world. "But he sent a few texts the day I was home. I just didn't have the energy to answer. Somehow he's always so extra."

"Tell me about it," I say, thinking of the jet of water hitting me in the neck.

"I don't even know him any more. He hangs out with all the idiots who are only interested in parties and getting drunk. He wasn't that superficial when he left, was he?"

"I guess you've both changed," I say.

"But he wasn't that way when he was younger, right?"

"He probably was a bit like that," I say. "But I think maybe he's very immature, very … ignorant. Somehow.

And maybe that's clearer now."

"Yeah. Ignorant. Good word," she says, scratching her tongue with her fingernails because one of my long hairs has found its way into her mouth. "Really ignorant about life."

"Really ignorant," I echo.

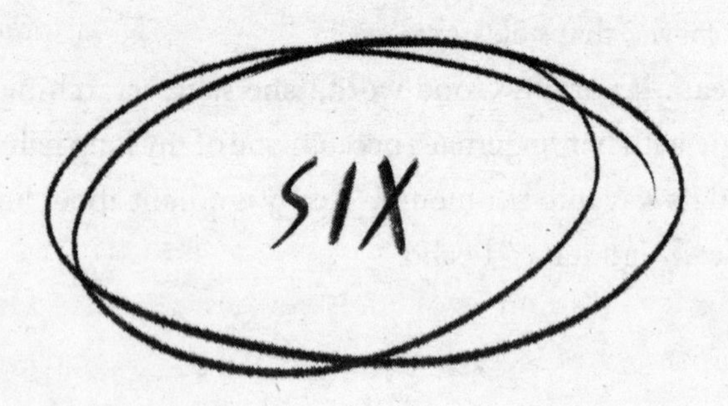

It's not my alarm that wakes me the next morning – it's the crying. When you've heard your sister cry as many times in your life as I have, you start being able to sort the crying into categories. Crying before school, crying before family parties. Crying that wants to be heard, crying that wants to be alone.

This is coming from the kitchen. I get up, go down the corridor, push the door open.

Mum's sitting on her haunches in front of Cecilie. My sister is crumpled up on a kitchen chair. Dad is standing in his underpants and shirt, fumbling with his tie. When he catches sight of me, he says a 'good morning' that feels like a sting, walks past me to the bathroom and shuts the door behind him.

My sister lifts her face from her knees and looks at me.

Her pale eyebrows are drawn all the way up her forehead, meeting in the middle in a soft arc of despair.

"I just want to go so much," she says, swallowing something that sounds like two or three mouthfuls of air.

"To the last day of school?"

The answer to my question is obvious, of course. On the other hand, it's less than a day since Cecilie refused even to discuss taking part, so in that sense nothing is obvious.

"I'd really like to try and go."

She uses the back of her hand to wipe something glistening from her cheek, then rubs her hand up and down her T-shirt.

"I really want to try," she says.

"Are you sure?" Mum is still crouching in front of my sister.

"No, I'm not sure." Cecilie buries her face back into her knees. "And Dad's just fucking furious!"

"Dad's not furious. He's only trying to look after you. That's what he's trying to do as best he can."

"But he doesn't understand!"

"*I* understand. It's hard when you really want to do something but you don't feel like you can."

"It's so unfair!"

"*Hugely* unfair."

My mum would be a good hostage negotiator. Even so, I think she's starting to see what Dad and I have already realized: that this is not one of those days when Cecilie will manage to leave the house. Her whole body is shivering.

Her face is mottled with effort and tears.

"You should do what you feel like today," says Mum. "Forget what Dad says. What do *you* need?"

"I don't know!"

But everyone in the house can see what she needs. My dad just can't stand to watch it any more, so he's run into the bathroom.

"Come on," says Mum. "Let's get you into bed. You're shattered." She sends a long-suffering, sympathetic look in my direction. "Cecilie hasn't slept since four."

"Half past three," sobs my sister. "And I don't want to sleep! I don't want to! But I'm just so tired."

Mum gets her to stand up. "If you want to go when you wake up, you can always text Astrid. She can come and pick you up. Then you can head over to school together. Right, Astrid?"

"Yeah," I say. "Just text me."

"See," says my mother, tucking Cecilie's arm beneath hers and starting to walk. "It'll sort itself out. If you fancy going when you wake up, you always have the option."

My body feels heavy as I ride my bike; I can barely pick up speed. My sister's tears are a wet, heavy bog and I'm stuck in it. I can't bear to think she's not coming today. That she's missing out on the last day of school. What else will she miss out on? Lately I've starting wondering that more and more often.

How my sister's life will turn out.

If it'll turn into anything at all.

As I bike down the avenue of cherry trees, I catch sight of my best friend. He's waiting for me outside the red-brick school buildings, checking his phone. The sight of him always puts me in a better mood. From a distance, he looks like a colourful set of traffic lights with his yellow bucket hat, his red 'I don't give a fuck about your diet, Susan' T-shirt and the bright green trainers.

"Ready to take a stream of piss to the neck?" he asks, squinting into the sun and fractionally adjusting his hat.

"*So* ready." I push my bike next to him as we walk towards the racks.

"Is Cecilie coming today?" He's using the voice he must imagine makes him sound casual.

I park the bike, bending over the lock as I reply.

"No."

"What? No way!" he says. "Then we're not getting chucked in the old pond!"

"Like she ever wanted to drag you anywhere."

On their last day of school it's tradition for the third years to drag first years to the pond and throw them in. It's usually something that happens to boys who've somehow misbehaved throughout the year – but girls stupid enough to show up wearing white T-shirts on such a day are at risk too. Luckily Jonas and I don't fit in either of those categories.

We set off towards the main entrance. At that moment, an old Volvo rolls into the car park. The passenger door opens even before it grinds to a halt. The first thing that swings out of the open door is a pair of purple Crocs, then the rest of Veronica comes into view. Jonas has stopped short beside me. I try to keep us moving by taking two steps forward, but he doesn't budge.

"Do you think she's got more pairs of Crocs at home?" he asks. "Maybe in … yellow?"

"I don't know. Come on." I drag him by the arm and he begins to move at last, but he's still staring at the car park, so I do too. Veronica gives us a wave, before leaning down and speaking to the driver, confronting us with an inescapable view of her arse in the slightly too-large jeans she always yanks up to her navel. Then she starts walking towards us at a pace that means we end up colliding outside the door with something that feels like a centimetre's precision.

We sit like this: me, Jonas, Veronica.

As she takes her books out of her bag, I eye her surreptitiously. She clearly doesn't tweeze her eyebrows, but she's got really good skin. Looks like the type that only gets a cute handful of freckles on her nose. The big glasses, the purple Crocs, the lack of make-up. She's going for an intentionally nerdy look but it only works for her because she's actually kind of pretty. Suddenly her head turns as though she caught me staring.

"Are you thinking the same thing I am?" She wrinkles her brow and glances down at herself, then laughs. "I think we forgot to wear white."

Nikoline and Fillippa are wearing tight white tops – an open invitation to be caught and thrown into the pond. We've all heard the rumours: how the third-year boys scour the classrooms for girls in white and chuck them into the stinking, algae-filled pond behind the school, so they have to wade out, soaked to the skin, and reveal their choice of underwear. It's so gross and degrading that there are girls who help keep the tradition going. It forces us to declare ourselves either as giggly airheads or prudes. The guys are ten times worse though – rude, sexist idiots. Their mums must be so proud.

During the last twenty minutes of the second class, everyone's starting to fidget. Nikoline and Fillippa clearly went to fix their hair and make-up in the break between the first and second lessons so they look good for the four seconds it takes the third years to grab them.

I've got my phone out on the table. Cecilie hasn't texted.

I can feel it radiating silence. The loneliness and frustration seeping from the blank screen. I text two hearts. She sees them straight away, but doesn't answer.

I write:

All you have to do is text!

I add:

Thinking of you.

At five to ten, the shrieking begins. It's coming from one of the classrooms further down the hall. Our social studies teacher frowns but continues talking about the far-reaching consequences of EU regulations regarding the curvature of our cucumbers.

"Sounds like someone's terrified," whispers Jonas.

"Or like a school shooting," whispers Veronica.

Around us, students are starting to turn to one another, cautioning everybody to put their computers and phones away.

Our teacher raps on the desk. "If we could come back to what can be done to—"

The door is flung open. It sounds like all the girls in the room are screaming except for me. Five guys with neon-green sweatbands round their heads and wrists run in and pump water in all directions before two of them leap over the tables, grab Nikoline and Fillippa and drag them away, despite what are supposed to sound like vehement protests.

"Yawn," says Jonas once they're gone. "Yaw-fucking-awn."

Our teacher sighs. "OK, then I guess let's just say thanks for this year and good luck with the exams."

We head down to the Bathtub. The noise of whistles and megaphones is deafening. Everyone's acting like a herd of disorientated sheep to the slaughter, pouring in the same direction while neon-clad third years sweep past, bumping into us with angular shoulders and damp water blasters. I stick close to Jonas, thinking it's a good thing Cecilie's not here.

I'm trying to get my phone out to see if she's replied to my texts when my feet are suddenly lifted from the ground. A pair of strong arms have grabbed me from behind round my waist.

When I twist my head to see who it is, I'm staring straight into Fillip's face. He gives a sinister laugh, wiggling the pierced eyebrow, before throwing me over his shoulder so my torso is hanging down his back. When I lift my head and look up, I'm gazing directly at Jonas and Veronica. Her eyebrows are pinched above her glasses and her lips move soundlessly as she tugs at Jonas's arm.

"Help me!" I say. "Put me down!"

But I can't even hear my voice in my own head; everything is drowned out by a load of people blowing on whistles.

Fillip begins to jog down the corridor, my head knocking against his lower back. Other third years catch up with us along the way, also with girls dangling down their backs like limp prey. My heart is hammering as I cling to Fillip's hips, trying to ward off the sense that I'm about to plummet to the floor.

"Put me down!" I say louder, more determined, and this time I hear my own voice, but I don't know who I'm even talking to – his arse?

We're outside in the fresh air now and the wind tugs at my hair, blowing it in front of my face and blinding me. Suddenly we're by the pond and the water and the sky swap places as he puts me down. I stagger backwards as I touch the ground, lose my balance and end up on my backside with a bump. So much blood has run to my head that my cheeks are burning and my pulse is throbbing hard behind my eyes.

There's already a whole gaggle of shrieking girls waist-deep in the pond. A third year in neon-green trunks has one leg planted in the water and another on land, and he's pushing the girls back in whenever one of them tries to wade out. Nobody is allowed out of the water until they've dunked their upper bodies and are ready to walk all the way back to school like Miss Wet T-shirt.

"Dip!" several of the boys are shouting. "Dip! Dip!"

I don't get what's going on here. Why they've taken me. I've never been with a third year, never drawn attention to myself, and I'm wearing a dark blue top that wouldn't reveal my choice of bra no matter how drenched it got. Maybe they got me confused with someone else. I get to my feet. Fillip's walking towards me, hands outstretched while he laughs.

"Stop!" I say.

"You can't stop it now."

"I mean it! Don't touch me!"

"You'd better learn how to be polite to your elders." He lunges at my wrists, grabbing one and starting to drag me towards the water.

"It wasn't even you I was talking to that day."

My voice is shaking. The skin of my wrist is hurting beneath his strong fingers.

"Doesn't matter," he says. "You should still learn to be polite."

"Fuck you, I am polite!"

"Ahahaha!" A machine-gun laugh. "Feisty, eh?"

A new group comes running down with screaming girls over their shoulders. It distracts me for a second, long enough for Fillip to seize my other wrist and drag me several metres towards the pond. I brace myself against the grass with my rubber-soled shoes but it's soft and my feet skid and tear up the soil.

"Just give up," he says.

"Let me go!" I sound decidedly scared and I'm furious he's made me come across like that.

"Guys! Little help over here!" he yells, and suddenly there's a guy two metres wide and two metres tall grabbing my legs and lifting me into the air. I try and kick myself free but all I can do is make the giant underneath me stagger a little.

"Shit, man, she's kicking!"

"Just get her down there!"

Then I set eyes on Kristoffer. He's seen me too. He's making a beeline for us as we totter closer to the edge of the pond and the sight of someone I know almost makes me sob with relief.

"She doesn't think it's funny," he says. "Put her down now."

"It's revenge, man," says Fillip.

"Pick one of the others," says Kristoffer.

"Fuck right off."

We're less than two metres from the water now. I can smell the musty algae and then my body reacts instinctively: I throw myself forward, using all my weight to make the giant lose his balance, and it works. I tumble down straight into Kristoffer's arms, throwing both mine round him and holding on tight.

"Hi?" he says, sounding surprised.

At the same moment, the other two grab me from behind, heaving at my legs so I'm stretched out at full length. I cling to Kristoffer and he tries to hold on, but the others are too strong. My fingers slip and I scrabble for purchase, tearing at

Kristoffer's T-shirt and digging my nails into his upper arms.

"Let … the fuck … go!"

They're laughing and groaning behind me. Then there's a violent jerk from their side and I lose my grip. I just about manage to grab the neon-green whistle around Kristoffer's neck, tugging so hard that the string cuts into his skin before it gives way and snaps. We all tumble to the ground. The two idiots start laughing hysterically.

"Your time of the month or what?" says Fillip. "You forget to stuff a cork up there? Is that why you're panicking?"

"Fuck you!"

I scramble to my feet, whirl round and start running back to the school buildings. The screams and the sound of spraying water are getting less and less distinct but then I hear laughter, someone shouting, asking if they need backup, if they can't handle a little girl by themselves. I don't look back. I just keep running. Only once I'm inside do I realize I'm still clutching Kristoffer's whistle in my hand.

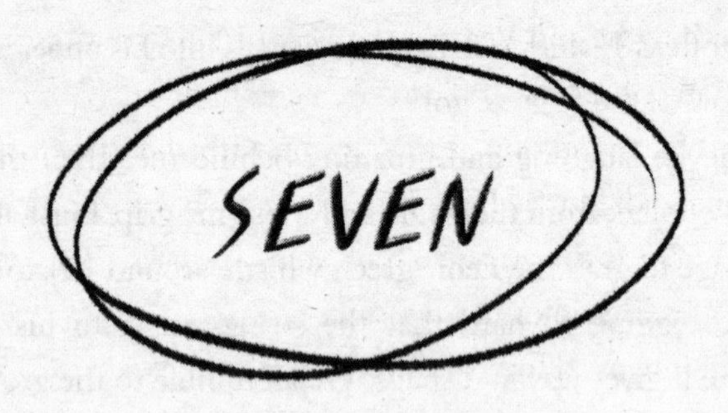

My body won't stop shaking as I reach the classroom and find my bag. The whole time I've been on the verge of tears but I manage to hold them in. I'm not about to snivel over something so stupid. I don't want to think about it ever again. Yet I still get the feeling I look like a downtrodden victim when Jonas and Veronica bump into me right outside the classroom.

"Are you OK?" Veronica gazes at me through her oversized glasses, making an attempt to take my hand, which I manage to dodge.

"Yeah, but I'm going home now."

"We'll make a statement," says Jonas. "File a complaint! It's not right – you can't just lob people in the pond. For one thing, it's sexist. For another, it's bloody dangerous."

I might have enjoyed his vehemence if it didn't sound like

something he and Veronica had cooked up together.

"Hang on," I say. "I didn't even end up in the water."

Veronica is staring at the whistle with the broken string in my hand. Hurriedly I stuff it into my bag.

"Who was the guy who took you?" she asks.

"Fillip. This idiot in my sister's class."

She frowns. "How'd you get away?"

"Kristoffer helped me," I say, and it strikes me I'd have ended up in the pond if not for him. But then I remember I'd never have been dragged down there in the first place if it wasn't for his brain-dead friends.

"Oh, Kristoffer…" says Veronica as though she knows something I don't even know myself.

"Of course he came to the rescue," says Jonas. "He's nuts about you. It's so obvious."

"No, he isn't." I tighten the strap on my bag.

"He always teases you when you guys bump into each other in the hall," Jonas says.

"What?! He says *hi*. Anyway, I'm not into people with such moronic friends."

Jonas and Veronica exchange a glance. He says, "The last time Astrid was sort-of-a-little-bit with someone was at the first school party last year, and that time she wasn't even—"

"Shut up," I say. "Or do you want me to start talking about you and Stephanie?"

We glare at each other. It's a look anyone would think was filled with hatred but in fact is filled with something that makes him my annoying brother from another mother.

"Aren't you coming back to the Bathtub?" asks Veronica, trying to break our staring contest. "We should probably … like … um … take care of you?"

"Sweet," I say. "But I'm not up for any more craziness today."

"Safe trip home then." She gives me something that doesn't get further than a half hug because my shoulder turns to block further bodily contact.

On the way out I see Caroline. She's wearing an orange dress; her hair is sprayed red and tied in pigtails. It doesn't exactly make her look less like a squirrel than she usually does. And she seems rather lost somehow, standing there in her silly clothes with a can of shaving foam in her hand, smiling at me.

"Enjoy being a clown for a day," I tell her.

My sister is sunning herself in the garden. Her long legs are outstretched and there's a stack of books on the table alongside a heap of peeled carrots.

"You feeling better, Eelie?" I ask.

"Yeah," she says. "I'm just sitting here in my little bubble, overseeing things. Can't you tell? I'm overseeing."

I love it when she's like this. All the things my sister truly is: funny, ironic, herself. I roll up my tight jeans as far as they'll go, then pull up a chair next to her so I can sunbathe too.

"You know I'm through, right?" she says. "They can't make me sit all the exams now. They can just fuck off with their absence rates and their rules. After the exams, I'll never, *ever* be answerable for *anything* ever!"

I can't help laughing because she's right: it *is* a minor miracle that she got through these three years. "You don't plan on having four kids and a husband who asks where you are? Or a boss?"

"No way. I'm going to be an unemployed cat lady for the rest of my life." She throws a glance at her phone. "Why are you home so early? Aren't the celebrations only just getting started?"

I snort. "Something dumb happened. I don't want to talk about it."

"Come on," she says, taking a crunchy bite of carrot.

I lean back in the chair and close my eyes a moment. Abruptly, I can feel how relieved I am the last day of school is over and I'll never have to pass Kristoffer in the hallway ever again. I'll never have to see any of the idiots he hangs out with.

"It was, um … the pond, you know?"

"What? They threw you in?"

"No, no, but Fillip tried."

"Fillip from my class?" She wrinkles her nose. "Why would he do that? Have you guys ever even spoken? That's just weird."

"I know."

"How did you get away?"

Sometimes I wonder whether my sister ever felt anything for Kristoffer, whether she's been in love with him at any point in her life. When I was a little kid, I used to get a bit jealous looking at them, thinking: *When we grow up, the two of you are getting married.* I thought they seemed like the perfect match but now the idea seems ridiculous. Because, if she did have feelings for him, she's kept it a total secret from me. And we have no secrets from each other.

Not till now.

"I just struggled free."

"Wow, you ninja."

I shut my eyes, feeling the sun warm my eyelids until everything goes red inside. "I wasn't really like a ninja. I was pretty much about to burst into tears and everything."

She laughs. I've still got my eyes closed, but I can't help smiling at the sound.

Nobody asks anything about the day that's just passed while we eat. Mum says things like: "There are more meatballs in the pan," and, "I think there's a good film on tonight," and, "I read that the water at the beach is already twenty degrees."

Sometimes I wonder what other families talk about. If they ever discuss important things, like what you want to do after school, when you're leaving home, what your dreams are.

After dinner, we wrap up in blankets, curl up together on the sofa and watch the film Mum mentioned. Dad sits in the old armchair, snoring. It's a pleasant sound. Like when I was little and crept into their double bed, and he would lie there, sounding like a big, friendly cave troll.

"Dad must be tired," says Mum. She's sitting in the other armchair, trying to keep one eye on the film while she reads a sheaf of documents from work. "Gosh, he really does snore."

She stares for a few seconds, as though she could stop him by glaring. "Thomas." She nudges his knee with her foot. "Thomas. You're asleep."

"What?" My dad opens his eyes, blinking in confusion, then closes them again.

"Yeah, and you're *snoring*," adds Cecilie, without taking her eyes off the TV screen.

He rises from the armchair, goes into the bathroom and starts brushing his teeth, a loud scrubbing noise drifting through the open door.

"Why don't we have a treat?" Mum stands up without waiting for an answer, goes into the kitchen and rummages in the cupboards, rustling bags of sweets.

"Shrimp," says Cecilie, her mouth against my shoulder. I can feel the damp warmth of her breath through the fabric of my top.

"What?"

"Nothing. I just feel safe right now." She burrows her nose into my upper arm. "At this exact moment, I feel genuinely safe."

Something painful pricks in my chest at her words. Like a small buzzing bee squeezing underneath my T-shirt and stinging.

"That's good," I say.

"Now I'm just starting to stress at the thought of all those shitty exams."

She lets her head drop into my lap, smiling a small, uncertain smile. Her body is very warm against mine. Her head in my lap is heavy. She wriggles her neck from side to side, the way she does when she wants me to play with her hair. My fingers move of their own accord.

"Will you help me?" she asks. "Cram with me? Like last year? After all, you're probably only getting tested on one subject max," she says. "Total bullshit."

I feel like asking her if she realizes that, by the time I graduate, I'll have been through exactly the same number of exams as her, so in that sense nothing is bullshit – it's just spread out.

"I'm sure I'll end up having to take English," she continues before I can say anything at all. "My typical shitty luck. And history too, I bet. Yuck."

"You should focus on getting through one exam at a time," I say. "The first chapter of the book. Focus on understanding the first sentence on the first page."

It's a tip from the mindful studying course Mum signed me and Cecilie up to last year: eat an elephant one tiny mouse-bite at a time. Or else it'll just sit on you.

"You're so wise." She turns her head and looks up at me, then prods my cheek with her finger. "Perfect, wise Astrid."

Mum comes back with a big bowl of mixed sweets. Placing it in front of us, she smiles at me when we make eye contact. I remember our plan to play croquet and have a barbecue tomorrow. Right now, it really does feel like we're going to have a proper family day.

Saturday turns out to be a bad day for croquet and barbecuing. Dad needs to go into the office and sort something out.

"Can't it wait?" asks Mum, although he's literally just said, "It can't wait." But she's still standing there with this look on her face, like a disappointed child.

"No, I'm afraid not," he says. "I'll be back in an hour or two."

"But surely … there must be someone else who can take care of it?"

"Someone I can call in on a Saturday?" He's looking irritated now. "It's my company, my responsibility."

A year ago, Cecilie asked me if I thought Dad was having an affair. It wasn't a real question. Just the kind she put out there, as though speaking aloud a thought that happened to flit by.

Our father definitely isn't the type to cheat. For one thing, he's an engineer. For another, the only people working at his company are men. There are five employees, who have been slogging away for eight years to establish a client base. I'm not really sure how it's going. He used to entertain us all the time with stories about weird electrical contraptions and investors who had to be plied with vodka to sign their contracts. He doesn't do that any more.

Once he's gone, Mum turns to us. "OK, well then, *we'll* just do something nice, shall we?" She jabs out the word 'nice' so hard, I'm almost afraid of it.

"I'm tired," says Cecilie, vanishing into her room. She lies there for the rest of the morning, dozing, and neither of us wants to disturb her.

The hours pass, clouds gather in the blue sky and suddenly the weather is grey and the whole thing seems like it will never happen, even though Dad called and said he's on his way home.

"We'll try tomorrow instead," Mum says to me. "There's supposed to be good weather all day."

It's a plan.

But then we wake on Sunday, and the plan feels dead before it's even come alive. Cecilie slept badly and is complaining about a pain in her back. I got up to pee at 3 a.m. and when I eased open her bedroom door I could see she was lying in bed, staring at her laptop. No sound, no music. She was just slumped there, with her face lit by the white glow of the screen, looking like a zombie.

"What are you doing?" I asked.

She shut the laptop with a jump.

"Sleeping," she said, pulling the duvet up over her nose.

Later Mum began to sneak around. There was whispering from Cecilie's room. Loud enough for me to hear them, not clear enough to understand what they were saying.

When I wake at half past eight, I lie listening to the silence before I get up. The house is completely quiet. I roll out of bed and go into the kitchen. Mum's hunched over a cup of Nescafé that's long since stopped steaming.

"Is there more water?" I ask.

"Just put it on to boil."

I take a mug from the cupboard and sit opposite her as the kettle begins to squeal.

"Rough night." She yawns. "Do you still think we should try and play a bit of croquet today?"

"Yeah. Don't you?"

"Sure." She gives me a smile. But I can tell part of her has had a change of heart overnight. Suddenly it's not our project any more but mine alone.

When I've finished my coffee, I go into the garden shed to fish out the croquet hoops and the brown leather bag of clubs. The sun is already high in the sky and the bees are humming in the flowerpots on the terrace. I start setting up a court on the lawn. Then I fetch a damp cloth and wipe the dirt and pollen off the garden furniture, put cushions on the chairs and open the patio umbrella.

Cecilie doesn't wake up till noon. She's hungry, asking for food in her room. I put cheese on a few pieces of crispbread and set the plate on her duvet.

"Why don't you join us in the garden when you've eaten?" I ask. "The weather's amazing."

She nods. Takes a tiny bite of the crispbread, but doesn't start chewing for another few seconds. Now her eyes are sweeping across the rolled-down blinds, the cracks of sunlight seeping through. Suddenly she changes her mind. "I'm really tired."

"You'll be less tired if you get some fresh air."

"Let's watch something." She puts the crispbread back on the plate, slides her whole arm round her pillow and flops heavily on to the bed.

"We can watch something later. Come on."

"Maybe later. I can't deal with this right now. I've only just woken up."

"You could take a bath, see if you feel any better?"

I can tell I'm skating close to the edge. The edge is where she starts taking what you say as a provocation. As a lack of understanding. It's in her face, like a tired, irritable mask.

But still I give the edge a nudge. I try shifting it a bit. "You'll feel better out in the sun."

"Don't nag."

She takes a bath half an hour later. I tell Mum Cecilie will be ready soon. She shakes crisps into a bowl, asks me to bring out cold cans of fizzy drink. Then I go and fetch my sister. She's sitting on the edge of the bed, clad in shorts and a T-shirt.

"Shall we go into the garden?"

She shoots me an exasperated glance but then pulls herself together.

It's purely for my sake.

I can see how every single movement has to do with my needs alone and nothing to do with hers. How she struggles to make herself stand, to walk. In the kitchen she slumps into a chair slowly, infinitely slowly, rocking her trainers over her heels. Then suddenly she takes them off again, studying the cracked skin on one foot.

"I've got really dry heels," she says. "Look."

"We can have a footbath tonight."

When we get outside, she pauses on the terrace, staring across the lawn and blinking her eyes. "What's that?"

"We're going to play croquet," I say, swiftly adding, "if we fancy it."

I scan her face for a curl at the corner of her mouth or any tiny hint of pleasure or anticipation in her eyes, but nothing happens. Today she's not my Eelie and for a moment it makes my stomach as tense and rigid as a stone.

"Just sit down and relax," I say. She sits.

Mum comes outside with her arms full of glasses, puts them on the table and smiles at us. "Let's just have a lovely time."

"What about Dad?" I ask.

"He's working."

"I'll go and get him."

My dad is in his home office, prodding the mouse round some densely written document on the screen. The blinds are angled so that a microscopic amount of sunlight just about filters through.

"Are you coming?"

"Are we playing now?" He looks up.

"In a minute."

"Come and get me when you're starting."

"We're starting in a minute."

"This'll only take two." He flashes me a grin before turning back to the laptop. I feel like going over there and slamming it shut, watching him react.

When I don't move, he glances up again and says, "Yeah, I don't think it's much fun sitting here working in the dark either, Astrid."

I leave.

Cecilie is curled up on the chair. She's drawn up her legs and is peering at her phone.

Mum's on the lawn, inspecting every single club. The red one, the yellow, the blue, the green. She holds them close to her face. I have zero clue what she's checking them for.

"Is he coming?" she asks, catching sight of me.

"In a bit," I say.

There's that shift in my mother's expression. Like when you flip dark lenses over glasses to shield yourself from something.

She says, "Shall we just get started?"

I want to say, *Are we giving up then? Are we really going to let him get away with sitting in there by himself?* But instead I ask, "Can't we wait for Dad?"

Her mouth narrows. "Of course."

"Shrimp?" calls Cecilie. "Could you please fetch my history book? I think I might have a bit of energy to study."

"OK, but we'll play in a minute, all right?"

She pulls a face in reply before I run indoors, find her history book on the desk and bring it back.

"Do you mind opening a Coke for me?" she asks as I hand her the book.

My sister hates the way opening a can makes her nails feel. I grab one, pull the ring and slide it over to her.

"Which colour do you want to be?"

"I don't care." She takes a sip of Coke.

I say, "We can play in teams? You and me versus Mum and Dad?"

"I might just watch." She picks up the book and holds it in front of her face.

Mum comes over. "You don't need to study now, do you, sweetheart?"

My sister ignores her.

I glance at my watch. It's been nearly seven minutes since Dad told me he'd be outside in two.

"I'll just go and see if Dad's ready."

Getting to my feet, I run back inside before Mum can say a word. He's still in his office, but now suddenly he's got a cup of steaming-hot coffee in front of him.

"Dad! You said two minutes!"

He gapes at me as though utterly taken aback that I'm standing there once more.

"What, you guys haven't started yet?"

"No, we're waiting for you!"

"Don't wait. Just skip my go. I'll catch up."

"So you'll just lose?"

"Someone's got to." He lifts the cup of coffee to his mouth and slurps.

I go back outside.

"Come on," says my mother, rising to her feet. "Let's the two of us play then, Astrid."

We play two rounds, me and Mum. She's red. I'm blue. I win. She's almost a whole round behind when I knock the ball through the last hoop.

"Congratulations on your victory," she says.

I think: *Were you even trying? Can you even be bothered to play happy families when it's just us two?*

We sit back on the patio. Cecilie is still buried in her history book, although nobody knows what they should be studying for until the subjects are announced on Monday.

I get the sudden urge to knock the book out of her hands. To hear the bump as it hits the ground, see her sulky face reshape into astonishment. Then I want to shake her so hard her teeth chatter and I want to ask her if she sees how senseless her behaviour is, how ridiculous. If she understands she's ruining everything by sitting there radiating what she's radiating. Sometimes I get thoughts about my sister that don't feel right.

Sometimes I wonder whether others would feel the same way about a person who has so much need of their solicitude. If other people get the urge to kick someone hard when they're already down. Squeezing my eyes shut, I try to think of something else. But of course you can't choose what you want to think about. Bad thoughts are like leeches, glomming on to your body and not letting go until they're fat and swollen with your blood.

I get to my feet. "Who wants to come for a walk?"

Mum glances at Cecilie before she says, "Honestly, I think I just need to put my feet up."

My sister doesn't answer, just clears her throat. A thin, tiny, guttural sound as she leafs through her book.

The harbour is teeming with people today. Friends, boyfriends and girlfriends, older married couples with dogs on leashes. People slurping ice cream and noisy kids catching crabs on the jetty, while their parents drink draught beer in the sun and eat greasy fish sandwiches from the kiosk.

Everybody except me has someone to walk with, someone to sit with.

I make for the longest jetty. Climbing out on to the big white stones, I sit down right by the water, taking off my shoes and waggling my toes in the open air. A big reddish-brown crab is shambling along on the sandy seabed beneath me, and one of the psycho gulls lands on a rock a couple of metres away and starts staring at my toes like they're tasty little sardines.

I text Jonas.

> Hanging out at the harbour, are you in? Just an hour. Urgent.

He sees my text but doesn't answer. That's something he's started doing lately. As though there's always something else that's more important than me. And it began after Veronica muscled her way in.

If she thinks she's going to be part of a trio, she's got another think coming.

If she thinks she can steal my best friend without a fight, she can forget it.

I send him two turds. He doesn't see them.

Then I get a text from Veronica.

> Hi, Astrid, want to come round my place and sunbathe in the garden?

I don't reply. Instead I text Jonas.

> Are you at Veronica's place???

Finally he answers.

> No, but are you up for it? Should be fun! Gonna crush some white wine!

Not in a great mood.

Can't you come down to the harbour?

Sorry, promised V I'd come over... Can't we hang out there? Turn that frown upside down?

Just forget it. Have fun.

My head is seething with sun and rage and upset plans.

Slipping my phone into my pocket, I turn my gaze back towards the sea. Today it's covered with big boats rocking on the water, the waves splashing against their hulls. Three boats down the line, a young man has clambered a few metres up an old mast, where he's fiddling around with some ropes. He's shirtless, wearing a pair of paint-spattered jeans, his hair almost bluish black in the sharp sunlight. It takes me a second or two to realize it's Kristoffer I'm staring at. Recognition gives me a funny kick in my stomach.

"Astrid?"

I turn towards the familiar voice. A short-haired woman is standing on the jetty, smiling down at me. She's wearing a sleeveless yellow dress and now she's waving her sunburnt arms. "It is you!"

I climb up over the rocks to the jetty, trying to compare this version of Kristoffer's mother, the one standing in front of me, with the one I remember: a plump woman running round the garden next to ours, hanging up the laundry in sagging joggers.

"It's so good to see you." Ellen gives me a hug, pressing me so close to her body I catch a waft of floral perfume. "Did you see Kristoffer's here too?" She points in the direction of the boat.

"What? No."

"Come on," she says, already on her way. "Let's go and say hello."

"I can't – I'm sorry." I stay rooted to the spot, trying to come up with a good excuse for not looking Kristoffer in the eye again.

"Is Cecilie with you?" she asks. "Are you waiting for someone?"

"No, but…" I don't have a good excuse and I'm not quick enough to fabricate a lie. Ellen realizes both those things.

"Come on then," she says. "Kristoffer's granddad is here somewhere too and I'm sure he'd like to say hello as well."

Kristoffer is still up the mast when I step aboard. From the deck, the boat seems even bigger than it did at a distance. The mast is several metres high, a thick white sail roped firmly round it. In the middle of the deck are a wooden wheelhouse and a set of steps leading down to the cabin.

"Look who I found!" says Ellen.

Kristoffer stares down at me. His legs are wound round

the mast and he's holding himself up with his arms. I raise my hand in a wave. Not a muscle in his face or body stirs.

"Come on, get down here," says Ellen. "And put some clothes on."

He climbs down slowly before jumping the last bit and landing with a thump. Ellen hands him a T-shirt she's picked up off the deck. He pulls it swiftly over his head. Then he squats down with his back to us and starts rummaging through a box of tools.

Ellen says, "Well, it's been ages, hasn't it?"

"We go to the same school." His voice is sullen.

"No, I mean *like this.*" She throws open her arms and laughs. "Like in the old days, when Cille and Astrid came round and invaded your playhouse all morning long."

Suddenly I'm glad he's got his back turned. I'm not sure I want to see the expression on Kristoffer's face when he's reminded of the days we used to sit there in our underwear, whispering about the difference between willies and front bottoms.

"You just sit down," Ellen says to me, pointing at three black folding chairs surrounding a battered camping table at one end of the deck. "I'll fetch us something cold." She heads into the cabin to get the drinks.

Taking my phone out of the pocket of my shorts, I place it on the camping table and sit down. The black plastic is burning hot against my bare thighs. When I shift my weight, the chair creaks. It sounds like a slow fart.

Kristoffer settles down opposite. Finally he looks at me. "Did you get home all right on Friday?"

For a moment, I consider opening with something friendly, maybe even thanking him for his help, but then I remember they were his friends.

"Mm." I turn my eyes to the water.

"People think you're a bit touchy..."

"People?" I look at him again. "What people? Your friends, you mean? It's not my fault they can only approach other people by humiliating them. Deal with it yourself."

He scrunches up his eyes slightly. "What am I supposed to deal with?"

"That your friends are arseholes."

"Wow."

"And you were by that pond too," I continue. "You were throwing girls in as well."

He says, "It's tradition. Don't you think some of the girls thought it was a little bit fun?"

"Yeah, the really feather-brained ones."

"You have a lovely way of talking about people."

The heat rushes to my face. "I'm just not into all that ... silly stuff."

At that moment, my phone buzzes. The screen lights up with a message from Jonas.

If you need to see me
that much, then come!

Kristoffer leans forward and reads it too as though it was the most natural thing in the world.

"Jonas," he says, swirling the name round in his mouth. "Is that your boyfriend?"

I snatch my phone to my chest. "No, it's my *friend.* Boys and girls can be friends, you know."

"I know that," he says, glancing up at the mast – or maybe it's his discreet way of rolling his eyes.

Then Ellen shows up with her arms full. She plonks the cans of fizzy drink in front of us on the table before touching my hair without a moment's hesitation and letting her fingers slip through it.

"Where's the short-haired, dungaree-wearing little troll I used to know? You always had holes at the knees. You always had those—"

"Mum," says Kristoffer, "drop the trip down memory lane."

"You look a bit different yourself," I say and instantly she touches her hips, her belly, asking if I really mean it, saying she's lost fifteen kilograms in the past year.

"And how is Cecilie doing?" Ellen takes the chair next to Kristoffer.

I say, "Good."

"Is she nervous about the exams?"

"Isn't everybody?"

"I'm not," says Kristoffer, and of course he says that.

"All this talk about hothouse kids – it's such a mistake,"

says Ellen. "You girls should just relax. Life's really not about grades at all."

"I know."

"But does Cecilie know that?" she asks. "Kristoffer told me—"

"Mum!" He glares, silencing her. And it's a good thing Cecilie's not here right now. She'd probably have punched Ellen for *real.*

"Well, she's certainly not a hothouse kid," I say. "She just … she definitely doesn't like taking exams."

"You know what? I've just had an idea." Ellen puts one elbow on the rickety table and rests her head in the palm of her hand. "It's just a suggestion…"

Kristoffer groans.

"No, stop it," she says, slapping at him. "When you've experienced something life-changing, it's a wonderful feeling being able to pass it on."

"Pass what on?"

Kristoffer stands up. "I'm going to take a piss."

"I'm doing this training programme," says Ellen once he's disappeared into the cabin. "As a meditation teacher. I was rushing round, doing everything for everybody at home and at work. But that's over now. I've started *being* instead of *doing*. Do you hear the difference?"

"I went on a mindfulness course once," I say. "With Cecilie. Is it kind of the same?"

"Not quite." She starts explaining something about the

difference between being and not-being, which I don't quite grasp. "I'd love to guide you through a meditation, if you think Cecilie might be interested?"

I smile politely, but in all honesty I have no idea what to say.

"I mean it," she says. "Ask her."

Kristoffer returns from the cabin.

"What about Thursday?" continues Ellen. "Half past seven? We can start with a cup of tea."

"Mum," he says, "you have got to understand that your hippie crap doesn't interest people. They're just being polite."

"He thinks I'm embarrassing," she says to me, patting his leg. "His friends call me Yoda. Isn't that sweet? So, shall we say Thursday?"

I think, *I'll never get Cecilie to say yes.*

"OK," I say, smiling. "It'll be fun."

Kristoffer's granddad, Sven, comes aboard a little while later. He must be at least seventy-five but looks in good shape, with a fierce sunburn and a thick white Santa-esque beard.

"Hey, I remember you!" he says, standing in front of the table and pointing at me. "Was it … Louise?"

"Guess again," says Ellen.

"Monika?"

"Her name's Astrid," says Kristoffer as though the name game is really getting on his nerves.

"Yes, that was it!" Sven slaps his thigh. "You were the playmate. Oh yes, I remember you clearly, you and the other one – what was her name now? Was *she* called Louise then?"

After I've told him my sister's name, he brightens and exclaims, "Well then, shall we have some schnapps, since we've got guests?"

Before any of us can answer, he's vanished into the cabin, returning moments later holding a dark bottle with a tattered label that's impossible to decipher and four small plastic cups that smell like coffee grounds.

"A toast then." Sven raises his cup to us.

It's home-made rosehip schnapps, and it burns first in the throat and then in the belly, until at last the warmth reaches your head.

"She liked that," he says in satisfaction as he watches me down the whole thing in one go. "Let's have another one!"

Worried he's going to pour a third, I only sip at the next schnapps. Then Kristoffer's granddad wants to know what I'm going to do with my future. I say I've got no idea.

"I always wanted to be a journalist," he says. "You've got to remember to be passionate about something while you're young, or you'll just grow old and full of regret."

"Dad, honestly," says Ellen. "You and all your silly warnings about the future. Let the young be young."

"And the old be old," he continues, pouring more

schnapps into Ellen's cup.

Sven is still standing. It occurs to me there's a solid chance I'm sitting in his folding chair.

"Thank you for the schnapps. I'd better be going."

"See you on Thursday," says Ellen. "Don't forget now. Half past seven, both of you."

"Thursday," I repeat. "I'll pass it on."

Kristoffer pushes back his chair and stands up the moment I make to leave. "Why don't I grab some ice cream?"

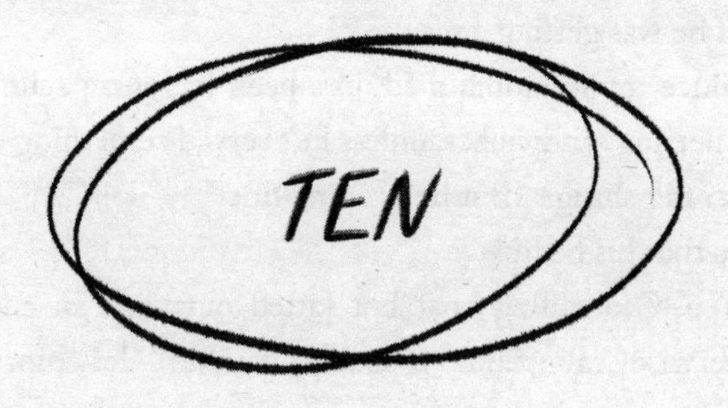

As we walk down the jetty, our shadows lead the way. His is large, mine smaller, and suddenly his shadow pushes mine with both hands.

"What are you doing?"

"Giving your dark side a little shove."

"Haha," I say. But there's something about the shadowy nudge that leaves me completely dizzy for a moment.

We keep walking down the promenade.

"I think I remember your granddad," I say. "Didn't he always used to sit in that old red velour armchair? He'd drag it into the garden when the weather was nice?"

"Good memory." He glances over his shoulder at the boat before carrying on. "Mum was worried about him the whole time we were in Greenland. If he was getting a proper meal every evening. If he even washed himself."

"If he was getting a meal…?"

"Since my grandma died, he's been living off schnapps and herring sandwiches, unless he's served something else." Kristoffer shrugs. "But he's coping fine."

"Is that his boat?"

"Yep. Old sailing boat but kitted out with an engine. Otherwise my mum probably wouldn't let him sail anywhere."

We pass a young couple with a big black Labrador in tow. It comes pelting towards us until they tighten the lead and Kristoffer takes a step closer to me.

"Still scared of dogs?" I ask.

It takes him a moment to answer, like he's considering whether he wants to show me a weakness. "Only drooling mutts from hell," he says, with a crooked smile.

And for a moment it feels nice walking next to him like this. The air smells of the sea and French fries and vaguely of his body: aftershave, fresh sweat. I wonder if he can smell me and what I smell like.

Then he ruins the moment by asking, "So what exactly is wrong with Cecilie?" And, before I can answer, "I know it's something psychological. I'm not stupid. Is she depressed?"

It should be a relief that he just comes out and says it instead of letting me get tangled up in a bunch of lies, but I still feel a jolt in my stomach.

"She has anxiety," I say. "It goes through phases. Right now, it's bad."

"OK." He doesn't seem surprised at all. "How long has she had it?"

"Since she was…" I try to count backwards. "Fifteen, I think. It started with this stomachache that wouldn't go away. Mum took her in for loads of tests but in the end the doctors said it had to be something psychological. They said she probably had seasonal affective disorder but it just never stopped. Then she began making a fuss about going to school and stuff like that. She's just too low-energy to do much in general. She can't cope with anything. She's just, like…" I need to blink a few times so I'm not overwhelmed by remembering something I'd almost forgotten – by thinking back to how it started. "Ground to a halt."

"But she's coped with high school," he says. "Or she soon will have anyway. Unless, of course, they're making her take exams in everything. Are they?"

"No, she just scraped through."

"That's lucky," he says, without looking convinced. "Feels like she goes home early a lot or vanishes in the middle of class. People say—" He stops himself, then continues anyway. "Everybody in class feels bad for her. Nobody thinks she's got it easy or that she's been skiving for a laugh. Just so you know."

"Good." My voice is weak. He shoots me a quick glance.

"I want to help. If you think there's anything I can do?" He says it like he genuinely believes there's something that can be done to help my sister. And in a way it's incredibly sweet. In another it's irritatingly naïve.

"Maybe I should have caught up with her, spoken to her more, but..." He pulls a face. "You know."

I'm not actually convinced I do. Sure, my sister isn't the type of girl whose desk you plop your arse on while you're munching a Snickers and asking how her crazy weekend went. But she used to be his friend. He could have said *something.*

"Don't worry about it." My voice sounds dismissive; that's good. "She's seeing a psychologist tomorrow."

"OK, so she's getting professional help?"

"Yeah." I don't have the energy to explain that she's been through counselling before and it didn't help much longer than the couple of weeks she was doing the sessions. "But when she's feeling bad, she basically just wants to be left alone. She only wants to spend time with me and Mum."

"What about your dad?"

We both move aside to dodge an older couple eating ice cream, so he doesn't see my face when he asks his idiotic question. When we're walking beside each other again, he says, "Your parents are still together, right?"

"Yeah. Dad's just not really part of that stuff."

"Part of what stuff?" he asks.

"I mean ... in a way I think he's kind of given up trying to understand it."

We pause outside the ice-cream kiosk.

"Don't you get pissed off?" he asks.

"With who, my dad?"

"Yeah. If he won't make the effort to understand?"

I say, "I don't know. It's just the way it is. You can't force people to understand something they don't."

"He's an adult. He's your dad. Of course he can. It's OK to make demands of him."

"Easy for you to say."

He stares at me for a long moment, like I've just given him the world's most complicated riddle. "I'm so done with people who can't be arsed to imagine what it's like inside my head." He takes a step forward, joining the long queue for ice cream behind a mother with a small wailing boy. "It's so lazy," he continues. "I'm not giving any fucking free passes to the people in my life who refuse to understand me."

"Oh. Right."

"And now you obviously think I'm a hypocrite," he says. "Because I never asked Cecilie how she's doing. But I really am trying to be a better person. I'm trying right now."

I honestly don't know what I'm supposed to say to that, so I just stare at him, but it doesn't look like it was an attempt to make me laugh.

"I want to understand other people," he continues, dead serious. "Why they do what they do. Or don't do."

I say, "But you're making it sound like it's an active choice whether to understand someone or not."

"What else could it be?" He moves forward in the queue, while I stay glued to my spot on the tarmac. "Why don't you just ask your dad what it is he's having such a hard time getting?"

The mum with the angry little boy has half turned towards us, clearly listening in while her child tries to wriggle out of her grip. My face is growing warm.

"It must be nice being you," I say. "If everything in your world is so simple."

"You think?"

"Yeah. And now I'm leaving."

"See you Thursday," he says as I turn my back.

Monday morning I'm with Cecilie, ready. We're each at one end of the sofa, computers in our laps, and I've got Jonas on Messenger. At ten o'clock the school will update its website, telling us which exams we're taking. It's the Ministry of Education that actually decides. The first years only sit one exam, the second years three and the third years six. My finger hits F5 to refresh every other second. F5. F5. F5.

Then it happens.

"Social science!"

Jonas sends me a storm of poop emojis.

I look up. Cecilie is as white as a hospital sheet.

"What did you get?" I ask.

Her voice is trembling slightly as she tells me. "Physics, French, biology … English and history."

"Isn't that … isn't that OK?"

"I'm supposed to wear my graduation cap after history," she says. "*Shit. Shit*!" Tears well up in her eyes.

I put my laptop on the coffee table and clamber over, hugging her and stroking her hair, which feels a bit greasy today. I'm looking at her features very close up – the red nostrils, the eyelashes that are soft and damp and free of make-up.

"It'll be fine," I say. "You'll manage."

"I'm so bad at history. I can never remember any of the dates. And I don't want to do a physics exam. My physics teacher hates me."

"Stop it. You're amazing at physics. You're a massive nerd!"

She smiles through her tears. I take advantage of the moment, the smile, to say, "And at the psychologist today you can unload all the shit you need to get off your chest. All the stuff that's getting to you. Yeah?"

She falls silent.

"You didn't forget it's today, did you? Mum's driving you at four, and I promised—"

She interrupts me. "I know."

Part of me wants to explain, to remind her how things ended last year.

"Mum says the psychologist is young?"

Cecilie wipes her face with her fingers. Rubs them hard along the skin beneath her eyes. I can feel her bristling at the idea of talking about it. The invisible, physical resistance that's surfacing inside her.

"You need to give her a chance," I say. "I mean, they're there to help you."

"Yeah, yeah." She sniffs forcefully. "But you try and imagine sitting opposite a stranger and being forced to talk about all your deepest thoughts and feelings."

I say, "No, it doesn't sound like fun."

There are lots of things I have a mind to add.

But I don't.

Mum calls at half past two to say she's leaving work, so we've got time to a have a cup of tea before she and Cecilie set off.

"She's sleeping," I say.

"Fine, we'll just wake her when I get home."

She comes through the door at a few minutes to three, asking how our day has been. I say it's been fine. I tell her what exams Cecilie's taking, what I'm taking. We let Cecilie sleep fifteen minutes longer while we drink a cup of tea standing at the kitchen table. Then we go into her room together. Mum opens the blinds a crack. My sister groans from the bed, flopping on to her other side.

"Sweetheart?" Mum sits on the edge of the bed. "It's time. You'd better get up now or we'll be late."

Cecilie doesn't move. My heart abruptly starts to thud as I see my mum's fingers sliding slowly, almost appraisingly, through Cecilie's greasy hair. I should have reminded her to take a shower before she went to bed, but it's too late now.

"Eelie?" I grab her toes at the end of the bed, giving them a squeeze. "I'll do your hair. Come on."

Finally, Cecilie rolls over and opens her eyes. "First I need to pee."

In the bathroom I set to work with the brush, untangling her hair and spraying in loads of perfumed dry shampoo, which gives her a coughing fit. She doesn't look at herself in the mirror. The whole time she's gazing down into the sink.

"We should set off now, girls." Mum's in the doorway.

"I need the loo first," says Cecilie.

"Didn't you just go?"

My sister shoots her a glare that makes her say, "Sorry, of course you're allowed to go to the toilet."

Cecilie shuts the door behind her, and I head to the kitchen with Mum.

"Are you coming?" she asks.

Last spring I nearly always did, which meant a whole hour of trudging up and down the streets until they were finished.

"If you think I should?"

"You don't have to. Only if you want." She smiles, sweating. I can see small dark patches blossoming underneath her arms.

"Of course I'll come," I say.

Two minutes pass. Three. We're listening for the flush but it doesn't come. I think we're both starting to wonder what's going on behind the closed door. Is she still standing in front of the mirror, gazing into the sink? Is she sitting on the edge of the bathtub, doing breathing exercises? At a couple of minutes to four, we go into the corridor and Mum knocks.

"Sweetheart? Are you ready?"

"No."

"It's nearly—"

"Don't rush me!"

"OK. But we need to set off really soon, OK?"

No answer.

We stay waiting in the corridor. Two minutes past four. I know the drive takes twenty minutes. Cecilie's appointment with the psychologist starts at half past. Mum knocks cautiously again. I go into the kitchen. The whole thing is like an accident in slow motion. I can't bear to watch, but I have to listen.

"Cecilie? We need to leave *now*."

"My stomach hurts."

"We'll get you some paracetamol."

"Not that kind of stomach pain!"

"All right. Well, what kind?"

"Could you please just get *away* from the door?!"

Mum comes into the kitchen. Her face is empty, as

though she's mislaid her expression somewhere en route from the bathroom. I don't know what to say. I start picking up the dirty coffee cups on the breakfast table.

Dad doesn't come home till dinner is nearly ready. Mum's at the stove; I'm laying the table.

"How did it go today?" he asks.

"I got social studies."

"Really? Well – that's great!"

I realize that wasn't what he meant at all.

He gives me a quick smile, scratching the stubble on his cheek. "And how about the psychologist?"

"I'm afraid we had to cancel," says Mum, grinding salt into a pan. "Cecilie had some trouble with her stomach."

"Trouble with her stomach?!"

"Yes, trouble with her stomach," she repeats calmly, putting the salt grinder back in place and picking up the pepper mill, clattering the saucepan lid.

"What are we up to now then? Three thousand kroner out the window – if we count the two missed sessions back in December?"

"Well, I'm sorry if it's the money that worries you most about all this."

"Of course I'm worried about the money," he says. "I have no intention of paying for a service we never use.

Surely you don't either?"

She doesn't answer, simply filling the carafe of water and passing it to me. I put it on the table.

Dad throws up his arms. "I'll go and talk to her."

"Thomas." Mum blocks the doorway. "She's not feeling well."

"I know," he says, emphasizing both words. "That's the reason it's so bloody important she has these sessions." He keeps glowering at Mum until she moves.

I set the last glass of water on the table. Then I slip out through the door into the hall. Leaning against the bookcase, I watch Dad rap his knuckles once against Cecilie's door before he opens it without waiting for an answer.

"What's wrong with your stomach?" His voice is strident.

I can't hear my sister's response.

"Yes, well, it's important that you go. Mum's taking you, so you're *not* alone."

He takes a few steps inside. I follow, getting closer to the room so I can see Dad. He's frowning now, listening to Cecilie's reply.

"No, I understand that but sometimes it's about gritting your teeth and keeping the commitments you've made. Take a bit of responsibility for your own life. We're supporting you as much as we can but you've got to play your part. You're nineteen years old, Cecilie. You're essentially an adult."

I can hear her crying now.

My heart is hammering. I think about what Kristoffer said, that understanding is a choice. But I'm not even sure I know what's going on inside Cecilie's head right now and I know I want to understand. There's just a part of me that *can't*.

Suddenly Mum bustles past me into the bedroom.

"There's no reason to start a discussion now." She perches on the edge of the bed but I still can't see Cecilie.

"What would you suggest then?"

"I think it's best we concentrate on one thing at a time. Right now, what matters are the exams. Astrid has her revision period now too – they're studying *together*."

I can tell that Dad is thinking something he can't say aloud.

"We can start the sessions with the psychologist after the summer holidays, if they're still relevant," says Mum.

Then he just leaves. Out of the room, past me, and through the front door. It slams shut behind him.

When I've finished brushing my teeth, I get into bed next to Cecilie. I can smell her tears on the damp bedclothes when I pull them up to my chin. The knot in my belly stirs. It clenches even tighter at the thought that my sister isn't getting any help. That we're all she's got.

"I can't do anything right," she says as we lie in the dark.

"Yes, you can."

"I'm like a child." She's crying.

"No, you're not."

"I hate myself. Why can't I just be normal?"

"There's nothing wrong with you."

But suddenly they feel like lines I've been reciting for years. I think I've got better at delivering them but in another way they're coming out with less and less conviction.

I hope Cecilie can't hear that.

It would be awful if she could.

I don't pass on Ellen's invitation until Thursday morning. There's no point doing it beforehand anyway – Cecilie can never make up her mind about anything that's more than a few days away.

"Meditation?" she says, looking like I've just suggested we take two weeks out of our calendar to attend a silent yoga retreat.

"It's supposed to be good for stress and stuff like that."

The last couple of days we've been trudging round the house like two zombies with textbooks. Joggers, no make-up, no routine. Cecilie's been all right. It's as if these shapeless days suit her. I, on the other hand, have a Jonas problem. We were supposed to meet on Tuesday to keep planning our interrail trip but I had to reschedule for Friday when Cecilie had a minor meltdown about some part of the physics syllabus she'd overlooked.

"What did you tell Ellen about me?"

"Just that you don't like exams." I pick at my hair, avoiding her gaze and hoping she won't ask what I said to Kristoffer. "It's mainly just a reason to see us," I add. "I think."

"Why?"

"I guess she thinks it might be fun?"

"But what if Kristoffer's home too?"

"Well, what if he is?"

Cecilie stuffs some hair into her mouth and sucks it. "Why were you on their boat in the first place?" she asks as though wondering suddenly how the story started – and it started oddly, I'll give her that.

"Ellen saw me at the harbour. And then she just invited me."

"Oh yeah," she says. "That was the day you were angry."

"What? I wasn't angry."

"Yeah, you were upset because I didn't want to play croquet. And then you marched out and didn't come home for two hours."

She's staring directly at me as she speaks. My eyes want to run away but I force myself to stare back, although I can feel my face getting hotter and hotter.

"I can sense stuff like that," she says. "When you've had enough of me."

"I wasn't really angry," is the only thing I can think of to mutter.

"Anyway, you'll have to come up with an excuse," she says.

"Say we're busy."

"It's the revision period. She knows we're free."

"Say we're ill."

"Both of us?!"

"Whatever. Just say we're not coming. Make up some random lie."

"Or we could just go and check it out?" I suggest. "Probably only an hour or so, right?"

"You really want to see Kristoffer, don't you?" She nudges me with her foot.

"I just think people should stick to the commitments they've made." I don't realize I'm sounding like an echo of my dad until it's too late.

"All right. Well, you can go then," she says sullenly. "If you really can't figure out how to say no to people."

I drag my feet that evening. Taking ages at the table while we eat, volunteering to load the dishwasher afterwards, lingering in the kitchen, watching TV. Flopping on to the sofa and starting to massage Cecilie's feet, although she hasn't even asked.

"Shouldn't you be off soon?" she asks, after I've massaged first one foot, then the other, and then switched back to the first.

Mum walks past with an armful of washing. "Off where?"

"Astrid has a date." There's a strange note in my sister's voice.

A little scorn.

A little pain.

"It's not a date," I say, sitting up straight. "It's Ellen, our old neighbour. She's invited me over for a meditation session."

"Ellen? Kristoffer's mum, you mean?" She looks a bit confused.

"Yeah," I say, and I get to my feet because I don't want her asking any more questions. "Shall I send your love?"

The moment Ellen opens the door, she lifts her head as though trying to see something behind me. "Didn't you bring Cecilie?"

"She wasn't feeling a hundred per cent."

"Not ill again?"

"Again?"

"Oh, Kristoffer mentioned she was ill on the last day of school." She lets me into the front hall. "But I'm so glad you made it anyway. How about a cup of tea before we begin?"

She notices my eyes do a quick sweep as she leads me into the living room, and says, "Kristoffer's not home yet."

"OK," I say, trying to sound genuinely astonished she thought that information might interest me.

Settling on the sofa, we drink tea that tastes like freshly mown grass. Their place is small and cave-like. So many potted plants are crammed on to the window sills that there's no sliver of a view. On the wall behind us hangs a gigantic abstract painting, shades of red, orange and deep black almost flung on to the canvas in long tongues of colour.

"That's awesome," I say, pointing. "I really like it."

"It's by a Greenlandic artist." She sips her tea. "Buuti Pedersen."

"Did you like living up there?" I ask. Then the reason they're back pops into my head: the divorce. "I mean, it's beautiful, isn't it?"

"Some parts of Greenland are so beautiful you can't even imagine it," she says. "You've got to experience it. Other parts ... not so much." Her eyes grow distant.

I get the urge to ask her the kind of questions you can't ask grown-ups. If she was happy when they lived next door; if she loved her husband; if she ever felt at home in Greenland; if that was what went wrong.

"Do you think Kristoffer misses Greenland?" I ask instead.

"I think he misses his dad." She pours more tea. Unfortunately. "But he's fitting in well here. Better than I dared hope. He has so many friends, I can't keep track of them all. He's always running off to parties. The only thing he needs now is to find himself a nice girlfriend."

I don't know what I'm supposed to say to that, so I say nothing, taking a few more sips of my lawn-flavoured tea.

"When you were kids, I had this silly idea that he and Cecilie would end up together. We'd have such a lovely time, proper chats about the old days, you know? We'd have that history in common. Instead, it'll be some strange, shy girl I haven't a clue how to talk to at the dinner table."

I say, "Mm," as though I totally get what she's saying.

"Do you know…" she begins, then cuts herself off, rephrasing. "Not to pry but Kristoffer never tells me anything. He and Cecilie are in the same class, and they used to like each other so much, so I thought—"

"But they were younger back then," I say. "People change."

She leans back against the sofa, studying me. "Yes," she says. "You're right there. People change."

When I've finally managed to empty my second cup, Ellen asks me to lie down on the floor. I position my body on one of the small white animal-skin rugs scattered like ice floes all over the room.

"Close your eyes," she says. And when I don't instantly obey: "Close them."

I didn't realize how weird it would feel to close my

eyes in a strange house. There must be some deep-seated survival instinct telling my body to be on its guard. I need to squeeze my eyes shut and remind myself the whole time to keep them closed.

"We'll start with some simple relaxation," she says. "Then we'll move on to the meditation."

A gust of air brushes me as she gets up off the sofa and moves somewhere else. Moments later, panpipe-like music wafts through the room.

"Be aware of the contact between your body and the floor beneath you," she says. Her voice is deeper and softer. "Focus on the breath moving throughout your whole body. Don't think about it – just pay attention. Breathe in. Breathe out. Every time you notice your mind has wandered, let go of the thought and return to the breath: your anchor. Thoughts are merely waves gliding through you, and you are the sea."

I imagine myself as the sea.

A great foaming darkness.

But it's all too silly for me. My thoughts keep clinging firmly to reality, refusing to glide anywhere. My mind turns to Cecilie, to what she said about being able to sense when I've had enough of her. And I wonder what she's doing now. If she's lying in bed or sitting in the living room with our parents. Maybe she's sad I left; maybe she feels I let her down by not just cancelling. And why is it so important for me to be lying here, pretending to be the sea on a cold floor in a strange house?

"As soon as you notice your attention has wandered from the breath and turned into thoughts, gently guide yourself back. Breathe in. Breathe out."

But of course it's fine if I want to do something without my sister. I know that. It's just that I can really feel the magnet right now, really feel how much she needs me.

"And now I want you to slowly direct your attention away from the breath and down into your stomach."

Stomach.

Arms.

Legs.

Feet.

My body is starting to feel heavy. Bit by bit, I'm left with nothing but the panpipes, and I find myself in a strange place where I can feel I'm awake but I've forgotten where I am.

"Astrid?" Her voice is soft but it gives me a slight start. I'm not sure how long I've been dozing. "You just lie there quietly and gather yourself. I'll go and boil some more water for the tea."

I sense the air move as she sweeps past. I hear the kettle in the kitchen, a faint clatter, a door opening. I don't feel like opening my eyes. Mostly I just want to lie here, caught halfway between being and not-being.

Then I get an odd feeling.

My eyes open.

"Hi," says Kristoffer.

He's lying on his side, less than a metre from me, his elbow against the ground and his head resting on his hand. Now he's laughing at the look on my face.

"How long have you been there?!" I sit bolt upright, my hand racing to my thudding heart. His eyes follow my hand, and I pull it swiftly back.

"A while. Sweet dreams?"

"I wasn't dreaming. Because I wasn't asleep."

"You were," he says. "You were practically smacking your lips in your sleep."

Ellen comes back into the living room with two cups of tea in her hands. She smiles when she catches sight of us on the floor. Then she pauses. "Why don't you take the tea upstairs?" she asks, holding out the cups as though they'd been meant for me and Kristoffer all along.

Kristoffer's room is under the roof ridge. The walls are sloping. There's nowhere to sit except his bed, but there's enough space on there for us both.

"I'm not drinking that," he says, putting his tea on a chest of drawers and settling on the bed.

"I've already had two cups," I say, setting mine down too. "Think that was enough."

"My mum doesn't get that not everybody dreams of living on wheatgrass and spelt," he says. "I'm having serious meatball withdrawal. A good Danish meatball, without any crap. You just can't get one in this house."

"Have you considered making one yourself once in a while?"

"I can't cook," he says.

"Then learn."

"I'm too lazy."

"Meatballs are the easiest thing in the world. I can teach you in ten minutes. Max!"

"It's a deal," he says, holding out his hand, letting it hang in the air until I shake it.

I don't quite know how we got here but suddenly there's a meatball date in our future.

"What are you in the mood for?" he asks, pulling his laptop out from underneath the bed. "You want to watch something?"

I'm actually pretty relieved by his suggestion – that he didn't think we were just going to sit here, goggling at each other, until we found something to talk about.

He peers at the screen, then looks back up. "How about *Grease*?"

"*Grease*?!"

"Isn't that every girl's favourite film?"

"You cannot call *Grease* a chick flick," I say. "You literally just can't."

"How can anybody not like *Grease*?" He smiles, looking a bit confused. "It's the ultimate feel-good film about high school, isn't it?"

"OK," I say. "For one thing: gender roles. The cocky guy who's always thinking about sex and the goody-two-shoes girl who only ever thinks about love? Why can't the *girl* think about sex and the *guy* think about love?"

"I feel like Danny thinks about both," he says. "Actually,

I reckon Sandy thinks about sex quite a bit too. Haven't you seen the ending?"

"The ending?!" I say. "Don't get me started!" But I already have. "Why does she have to change? Why isn't she good enough as she is?"

"She does it for his sake. You don't think that's romantic?"

"You think it's romantic that she has to change for *his* sake?"

Kristoffer shrugs. "I just think he wants her to show that she's into him, because the whole time she's been acting like she doesn't."

"So, to get a guy to love her, she has to change the way she dresses, perm her hair, take up smoking and start acting all 'come and get me'?"

"Jeez, it's a happy ending," he says.

"It's crazy sexist! And loads of teenagers still watch that film, even though it's forty years and one Me-Too revolution too old."

"Shit," he says. "Maybe we should just watch *Winnie-the-Pooh*?"

"Anything but *Grease*."

"Yeah, I got that." He sounds faintly irritated.

At that moment, his computer starts playing the Skype ringtone. He hits accept, turning the screen away from me.

"Hey there ... so. Had a good day?"

I have only a vague memory of Kristoffer's dad. It was always Ellen or his granddad who was home, but I still recognize the voice: a slight accent, a kind of melody in the words.

"I've been studying on the beach. But hey, Dad – I've got a visitor."

"Who?"

Kristoffer looks at me over the laptop, maintaining eye contact for longer than seems polite, given that his dad's on the line.

"Someone from school," he says at last, his eyes flicking back to the screen.

"Shall I call you later?"

"I can just call you. Tomorrow."

"OK. Talk soon then. Have fun, eh?"

Kristoffer shuts the computer and slides it underneath his pillow. Evidently it was *Grease* or nothing. Now, abruptly, he seems restless. He gets to his feet, goes to the sloping window and opens it wide.

Divorce isn't especially familiar territory for me. Jonas's father died when he was twelve, but that's completely different, and in my whole family there's only one uncle and aunt who aren't together any more. I get that it must leave a mark when your mum and dad split up, but I'm not sure how big.

"Do you visit your dad much?"

"It takes six hours to fly to Nuuk so…"

"So not that much?"

He doesn't answer. Making for the narrow chest of

drawers, he opens one and rummages for something before turning towards me with a chessboard in his hand.

"What are you doing?"

We're sitting cross-legged on the bed with the board between us. His elbows are resting on his knees, his head supported on his fists. Now he glowers at me, pulling a serious face.

"What do you mean?" I can't help laughing.

"You've just put yourself in check again!"

"OK, then let me give it another shot…"

"*Again,*" he says. "Again I'm letting you cheat."

I move the rook swiftly back so that my king is protected, dispatching my knight instead. "There we go."

"Should we not have just watched something?" he asks, moving his queen forward. "Checkmate. And you're not allowed to cheat this time."

"So now I've just lost?!"

"Now you've just lost. Twice." He sweeps all the pieces off the board and starts putting them back into the little leather bag.

"Who taught you to play chess?" I ask. "Your dad?"

He says, "No one. It's pretty much impossible not to beat you."

"Funny."

"The winner gets to decide what we do next," he says. "So now we're watching *Grease*."

I don't protest, just lean my back against the sloping wall. He does the same.

The film flickers past on the computer screen. It's just as bad as I remember. But I kind of love to hate it. I point out all the gender stereotypes, telling Kristoffer all the stuff that bothers me about the plot and the morality.

He listens. Says, "OK," and, "Right," and a long drawn-out, "*Errr…*" when he doesn't agree.

Then suddenly he yanks the duvet up and tucks it carefully round my legs, over my stomach.

"I'm not cold," I say, kicking it off.

"The point of wrapping up in a duvet during a film isn't to stop being cold," he says, stuffing it back round my body the way you'd put a stubborn child to bed. "The point is to be cosy. Maybe you didn't know that?"

I elbow him. He elbows back. We keep watching, and after only a minute or two he shifts closer, but slyly as though he's just trying to find a more comfortable position. I keep an eye on every single movement. Every single millimetre of the journey his hand takes over the duvet on its way to mine. It starts to feel like we're watching a film neither of us is seeing.

His breathing.

My breathing.

Like uneven rolling waves.

Then my phone begins to buzz. It's in my trouser pocket and my whole leg hums with every vibration. I take it out, see Cecilie's glowing face on the screen, put it on silent and toss it on to the bed. The call ends, but after only a few seconds the phone lights up again. I try to ignore it, staring at the film. At last the screen goes black. But a minute later it lights up once more.

"Aren't you gonna get that?" says Kristoffer. "Seems important."

It isn't. Trust me.

"I'll just text her." I type quickly, angling my body so that Kristoffer can't read it. As I'm typing, I get a text from Cecilie:

Call me now!

I hesitate for only a second before throwing the duvet aside and shifting on to the edge of the bed. "I need to go."

"Why? What's going on?"

All of a sudden, I'm incredibly annoyed by the whole situation. Like Kristoffer has any right whatsoever to know what's happening in my life. Like Cecilie has any right to demand I come home.

"Nothing. I need to go, that's all."

He juts out his bottom lip. "But, Astrid, I was looking forward to you analyzing the ending for me."

"You'll just have to work it out for yourself."

I don't call. I just cycle.

My parents are going to bed when I get home. We say goodnight, and I use the bathroom. The door to Cecilie's room is closed and when I push it open she jumps. She's sitting in bed with her laptop in front of her but now she whips it shut with a click.

"Did you not see I called?!" Her cheeks are flushed. "I got the nastiest feeling something had happened to you. That you'd been knocked down or raped!"

"I'm fine."

"Why didn't you pick up?"

I don't have a good answer to that but my brain comes up with something lightning fast: "I put it on silent, then forget to take it off again."

"Was Kristoffer there?"

"Mm."

She shoots me a glance.

I say, "I'm just going to brush my teeth." But as I stand in front of the mirror, scrubbing, she appears in the doorway.

"What were you doing?"

"Meditating."

"For three hours?!"

"We watched a film too."

"So it *was* a date?"

I put my toothbrush back in my mouth and gesture with my arms to indicate she's mistaken, but she just widens her eyes as though she doesn't understand. I spit, rinse, lift my head and catch sight of my sister's face behind my own in the mirror.

"He wanted to watch *Grease*," I say. "I mean, *Grease*? Of all things! Really, really crap taste in films." My voice is much too loud.

She stares at me in the mirror for a few long seconds. It feels like she's seeing right through me. Finally she says, "He's very random with girls."

"Random how?"

"Just … random. Sleeps around."

"OK." I get a weird sensation in my body. Like I'm hovering near the ceiling, watching us from above, me and my sister. This conversation.

"I just don't want you to get hurt."

"It wasn't a date. I told you."

Cecilie goes back into her room. I follow. She gets in bed and pulls the duvet all the way up to her chin, looking at me with big eyes. I swallow a lump of guilty conscience and sit down beside her. "How was your evening?"

"It hurts like hell when I breathe. It really feels like I've got knives in my back."

"Ouch."

"And Dad's still angry I didn't go to the psychologist."

"Dad always seems angry and stressed because of work." But I know for sure that's not the whole truth.

"It just feels like I'm the one ruining things for everybody in this family." She turns her gaze to the ceiling. "It's my fault Dad is angry and it's my fault Mum has to take so much time off work. Everything is *my* fault."

"Mum and Dad will always be there for you," I say. "No matter what."

"Sometimes I think it would be easier if I just dropped out of school. Then you guys wouldn't always have to be fussing around me. I could use the time to get better. At my own pace."

"But all you need to do now are the exams," I say. "That would be –" I'm about to say *totally insane,* but change it to – "annoying."

"I can just feel the thought of the exams stressing me out like crazy, now they're getting closer. And it's making my anxiety go nuts."

"You'll get through it," I say.

"I could maybe do the make-up exam in August instead. Then I'd have more time to study."

"Hang on," I say. "We're cramming together. It's been going pretty well so far, hasn't it?"

"You think?"

"Yeah. You're good at your stuff. You just have to get used to talking about it in front of other people. We can do some role plays. I'll be the teacher and the examiner."

"OK, maybe," she says. "Tomorrow?"

"Ah, I'm meeting up with Jonas at eleven."

I have to bury my nails in my palm when I see her face fall slightly, as though she'd forgotten. Now she shifts in bed.

"Will you stay until I'm asleep? We can do that exercise where you transmit your breathing to me."

She pushes the duvet aside. I climb in next to her. We lie side by side, counting, until we start breathing in the same way, the same rhythm.

I used to feel like we were twins.

Now suddenly I feel like I'm growing apart from her.

I meet Jonas at the Harbour Café at eleven. I've always thought of it as our usual place, but standing there it strikes me it's been several weeks since we were last here.

Our meet-ups tend to start with a slurped cappuccino and a gossip about some of our classmates before we tackle the tough stuff, but we haven't even ordered or found a spot in the sun outside before Jonas says, "I think we should invite Veronica to come interrailing with us."

I need to act like I haven't heard him. My heart begins to hammer and I feel almost cross-eyed with shock as I nod my thanks to a mother with a pram who signals that we can take her table. Once we're sitting in the sunshine in our wicker chairs, he continues. "She's not doing anything all summer."

Luckily the waitress appears at that moment. She smiles

and welcomes us, asking if we're here for lunch, if we'd like to see the menu.

"Two cappuccinos, please," I say. "With extra foam."

"Sure."

"I'll have an elderflower water instead," says Jonas. Then he looks at me almost apologetically, saying, "It's freaking hot."

"One cappuccino with extra foam, one elderflower water coming up," says the waitress before she disappears, as though she really wants to rub in our differences.

Jonas tilts his head. "What do you reckon?"

"About what?" I try not to sound angry but now there's a wasp buzzing round my head and I have to slap violently at it.

"Veronica. Interrailing."

"You want to invite Veronicaraptor on a trip the two of us have been discussing since forever?"

"Can you please stop calling her that?" He sighs. A deep, tired sigh that isn't his usual style at all. "She just seems a bit lonely."

"She seems desperate."

"Come on," Jonas says. "You know it's not easy joining a new class."

"Are you kidding? She started in December." I count on my fingers for him. "December, January, February, March, April, May, June. It's been seven months!"

"Yeah, but we're the only people she talks to – she doesn't

speak to any of the others. She's a good fit for us," he says, which is a lie.

Veronica might be a good fit for Jonas, and Jonas might be a good fit for Veronica, but nobody is a good fit for Astrid any more.

"Will you at least think it over?" he asks.

I grunt a "hmm", which he can interpret however he likes.

"So, what, are you and Cecilie just sitting at home, studying?" he asks, using his casual tone of voice.

"Yeah. You're probably doing the same with Veronica?"

"We've only studied together one afternoon." He scratches at something that looks like a dried coffee stain on the table. "Things any better with Cecilie?"

"She's coping."

The waitress comes over, carrying a tray with our drinks. Jonas's glass is tall and thin and clinking with ice cubes swimming around in the golden liquid. My cappuccino cup is small and wide, a fat, wobbling wave of milky foam on the top. Jonas says thank you and takes a big sip from his glass. I say nothing. I can't even manage a smile at the waitress when she discreetly tucks the bill under the beach pebble painted with our table number.

"OK, you want me to be completely honest?" he says. "Somehow it just seems safer to be travelling in a group of three."

"That's something a mum would say. You'd never say anything like that."

"I just mean if…" He stops himself. "What if something happens, and you cancel?"

"Why would I cancel?"

"What if something happens with Cecilie? What if she's doing so much worse you feel like you have to stay home?"

It's like watching your best friend transform into an elephant and deliberately tread on your smallest and most vulnerable toe.

"I won't cancel," I say. "No matter what."

"OK." He gazes out across the water.

I stick the spoon into the cappuccino and stir it round and round. "But then maybe it's a bad idea to plan anything today. If you're thinking she's going to come, I mean. Maybe she won't like the route we choose. Maybe she'd rather go to other countries."

"She's crazy about seeing Budapest," Jonas says.

I stir faster. Some of the foam spills over the edge. "So you've already discussed it with her?"

"Kind of." He empties his glass of elderflower water before continuing. "But you need to be OK with it, of course."

"I've not really got much choice now, have I?"

He looks down at his hands for a moment. "It's been really difficult for me to say all this. I hate conflict. You're still my best friend, OK? I just think Veronica is really nice. Very genuine."

"Very genuine," I repeat.

"Being with her always puts you in a good mood, you know?"

I refuse to respond to that. My pulse is thudding simultaneously quickly and slowly, as though I can follow every single beat hammering in my temples.

"At least think it over," he says.

I gaze out across the sea, drinking my cappuccino. The milky foam settles in a thick bow on my upper lip before I lick it off with a swift flick of my tongue.

"Um. You've also got something … there…" Jonas points to his own upper lip. I wipe mine hurriedly with the back of my hand.

We sit for a while. I try to come up with something to talk about. Something we even *can* talk about.

Right now, it feels like he's lobbed a bomb into our friendship. The tiny, budding urge I felt when we met to mention Kristoffer is dead and buried now. I'd rather admit to masturbating with a shower attachment than tell him about last night.

Jonas takes out his phone.

We've never been the kind of people who sit opposite each other with our phones out.

But now I do the same.

The revision period suddenly feels endless. I start wondering about things I've never spent time wondering about before.

Like what you can really expect of a best friend.

What I'm going to do for the whole of second year if Veronica and Jonas become an item.

What falling in love actually feels like.

It's super impractical to start wondering about stuff like that when you should be concentrating on revision. There are eleven days till Cecilie sits her physics exam and fourteen until I take social studies. I'm not nervous about it. I do well at school, I keep up during the year, and I have a computer full of Google Slides from class and a stack of handwritten notes. Cecilie, on the other hand, has gaps in her physics material – lessons she hasn't attended, notes she's never taken.

"Why don't we try a role play?" I ask, after we've spent an hour trying to make her thin sheaf of physics papers grow. We're sitting in the kitchen, it's Saturday morning and our parents are out shopping.

"Let's pretend I'm the examiner," I say. "And the teacher."

My sister's hands, holding her physics book, begin to shake. It looks exaggerated. It's like giving an actor a cue – "Shake!" – and then she shakes.

"We're just pretending," I say.

"Can we stop pretending?"

"We agreed we'd try. And it's good to practise."

"Even the thought makes me go nuts. For real."

"You'll manage. It'll be fine." I point at her. "You got this!"

There's only one person in our family who's allowed to tell my sister she can cope with stuff without her biting their head off, and that's me.

"OK, then let's begin." I clear my throat. "Good morning, good morning, Cecilie. Why don't you tell us a bit about quantum physics? To be specific –" I skim the sheet I've just plucked from the top of her physics notes – "quantum leaps?"

She hides her face behind the book, holding it up so I can't see her. Several seconds pass. Maybe half a minute.

"Do you need to put on that masculine voice?" she says, still hidden behind her book.

"You'd never say that to an examiner."

"Why did you start with the hardest topic?"

"I don't know anything about physics. Shall we start with

something else instead?"

"I can't take you seriously with that voice." She pokes her nose above the cover and I can tell from her eyes that she's smiling. She's dragging the time out even further. Going cross-eyed, shifting her eyes slowly from side to side.

Why am I sitting in here with you? I think. *Why am I not with Jonas, hanging out and revising my own stuff?*

"OK, then let's drop it." I put the piece of paper on the table and get to my feet.

"Don't be angry!" she says.

But I'm not angry. I'm something else, something whooshing round my body. It's not just my sister, it's the house itself, the kitchen, the smells, everything, that make me feel trapped. I think she can tell.

"OK, I'll be serious now," she says. "Sorry, sorry. Hmm … quantum physics."

"Quantum leaps," I correct her, sitting back down. At that moment, my phone buzzes. The message is gleaming on the screen with the name of the sender: Kristoffer. I snatch the phone up.

> You forgot to take your water blaster home on Thursday.

"Who is it?" asks Cecilie.

For a moment, I consider saying it's Jonas. But then I get this overwhelming sense that she caught a glimpse of the name. "Kristoffer. Something about the water blaster."

She makes no comment, and I look back down at the phone, typing a quick reply:

You were the one who forgot to give it to me.

He answers straight away.

So when are you coming to pick it up?

Why don't you bring it over yourself?

Fair enough. When do you want me to come over? :)

I can feel Cecilie observing me as my fingers glide rapidly across the screen.

You can just put it in the shed whenever works.

OK, the shed. Got it.

I feel like flinging my phone at the wall just to stop myself writing any more dumb crap.

"You don't think he's a little bit into you? Just a teensy little bit?" Cecilie's looking at me, so I have to stare back down at the piece of paper.

"Because I did some meditation on his mum's floor?"

"You also watched a film with him."

"Shall we keep going?"

She hesitates a moment. Starts picking at the spine of her book. "You know it was Kristoffer who gave me my first kiss, right?" she says. "That time you were in bed with pneumonia for two weeks and we could finally be alone in my room."

"Do I look like I care? Can we keep going?"

She stares at me. I stare back.

Then an ugly thought crosses my mind, one I have no desire to think: *Yeah, you got a kiss, and it was the first and last time you kissed anyone. You were twelve. Twelve!*

"Tell me about quantum physics," I say, brandishing the piece of paper in front of her face. "Quantum leaps. Come on."

Sunday morning I wake early. When I go into the kitchen for a glass of water, my dad is lacing up his running shoes.

"You coming?"

He starts warming up for his run in the way fifty-year-old men do: stretching his legs, stretching his hips, small eager hops on the spot. Last year my dad ran a half-marathon. His goal is to do the marathon in Berlin in two years' time.

"They're predicting rain later." He darts a glance out of the window at the cloudless sky.

My dad likes to say his runs are his personal breathing space from existence and I'm pretty sure that includes his family. Us.

"You coming?" he repeats.

"OK," I say quickly, before he can change his mind.

We start hard, running side by side down the streets at a pace that pushes us both. Only once we reach the fringes of the woods do we slow down a bit. After a couple of minutes, I need to stop and walk. The air is thick with the scent of fir and moss. The forest always reminds me of when I was little and we'd go for walks, the four of us hunting for barrows, on the lookout for a good place to eat packed lunches or pick mushrooms. Back then, we still knew how to be a family.

"You're a strong runner," I say.

"Well, it's important to keep in shape." He pats his chest. "Good for body and soul."

"I prefer swimming. Remember the time we went to that father-child swimming thing?"

He smiles. "You two were incorrigible. And I couldn't get you out of the sauna once you were in there."

Suddenly I get an idea. "Isn't the pool usually open late on Thursdays? Till eight?"

"Thursdays I always work late," he says as though warding off my suggestion before I've even made it. "But I'm glad you came with me today. Actually, there's something I'd like to discuss with you, Astrid."

For some reason, my belly twists.

"I just want to make sure we're on the same page. We *need* to get Cecilie through these exams. There is no alternative." He gives me a look. "It's like with sports. You don't get results if you don't push yourself a little bit. And she does need to finish school. She needs to experience success. It'll give her a springboard so she can go out into the world and *do* something."

"Yeah," I say because I think he's right. I really do. It just doesn't seem especially realistic to imagine my sister ever climbing on to a springboard of any kind.

"What does she think about all this?" he asks.

For a moment, I consider suggesting he ask her himself. But then I remember the day last week when Cecilie told me she was contemplating dropping out. Dad would go mental if he knew she was so much as thinking those thoughts.

"I'm not really sure."

"But what about all the hours you spend with her every night?" he says. "Don't you talk about anything?"

"She's not doing so great."

"But she can do it easily. She just has to learn to believe in herself. The anxiety she's feeling is nothing but thoughts and physical sensations running riot."

I've heard him say exactly the same words before. Not to me but to Mum. It was during an argument, and he also said something about not wrapping people in cotton wool, which made Mum walk outside and sit alone on the bench at the bottom of the garden for a whole hour.

"I hope she'll get better soon," I say.

They're completely empty words, almost meaningless, but I feel like I need to say them. To defend my sister somehow.

"I'm afraid hoping doesn't change anything," Dad says. "These things take work. But you already know that, of course. We're a lot alike, Astrid. I see so much of myself in you."

He looks at me with eyes full of tenderness and pride and then he smiles.

It feels like the worst form of treachery against my sister when I smile back.

We drop by the bakery on our way home. As we head through the garden gate and past the shed, I catch sight of Kristoffer. Standing with his back to us, he's sliding the neon-green water blaster on to one of the top shelves.

"What the hell – is that Kristoffer?!" says Dad.

Kristoffer turns with a start, but smiles when he sees us.

It's not often my dad swears – it almost never happens – but now he does it again. "Christ, I've not seen you since you were a little squirt. And now you're lurking around in our shed!"

He sounds pleased. I can tell I'm glad to see Kristoffer too – I'm not even embarrassed to be standing here, all sweaty and red in my running gear, the bread under one arm, while he's smartly dressed in dark jeans and a grey jumper.

"I just came by to drop off something I borrowed from

Astrid … Cecilie," he corrects himself a second later.

"Why don't you come in and have some breakfast?" asks Dad.

"Sounds good but I've actually got to head off."

He slips his hands into his pockets. There's something slightly awkward about him that I've never seen before.

My dad looks from me to Kristoffer, then he grabs the bread from under my arm, saying, "I'll go inside and shake those two sleepyheads out of bed," before disappearing down the garden path.

We're alone.

My heart is pounding.

I say, "Thanks for bringing it over."

"Yeah, well, I was on my way to a friend's place anyway. Going to wake him up with a surprise brunch. It's not far from here. So…" He takes his hands out of his pockets, then stuffs them straight back in. "How's the revision going?"

"Social studies is going fine," I say. "Plus me and Cecilie are studying quantum physics and relativity theory and all that, so I'm going to learn a whole load of stuff this summer."

"You're doing her course material too?"

I don't really know what to say to that.

"OK, well, what have you learned so far?" he asks.

"That I'm not going to be in the top set in physics."

"What?!" he says. "That can't be true. A smart girl like you?"

I ignore his granddad impersonation. "Yesterday, for

example, she was trying to explain what a quantum leap is. It didn't go so well."

"Quantum leap? That's easy."

Kristoffer goes back into the shed, quickly scans the shelves and reaches for the old tin of coloured chalks, which is still in the same place it was when we were kids. Then, crouching down outside the living-room window, he draws a big round circle on the patio, colouring it in until it's one large blue disc. He adds some uneven, slightly wavy rings around it, each one bigger than the last.

"Come over here," he says.

I go and stand beside him, a few steps from the large chalk drawing.

"This is the nucleus." He points at the blue circle.

"What nucleus?"

"OK," he says, wrinkling his brow. "I'm starting to understand Cecilie's problem."

Part of me wants to give him a shove or a slap but now we're so close I can't make myself do anything like that.

"Sorry, guess I should be nice." He points again. "The nucleus of an atom. OK? And an atom is—"

"The smallest unit you can divide an element into," I say.

"Good. And inside the nucleus there are neutrons and positively charged protons, then around the nucleus there are electrons orbiting. They're negative."

"The nucleus of the atom," I repeat. "And some stuff orbiting it."

"Specifically...?" He looks at me as though wondering for a moment if I'm remotely teachable, but then he grabs my shoulders and manoeuvres me so I'm standing on the innermost ring around the nucleus. "All right, Astrid, you're an electron. You're negatively charged. And you're constantly circling round the nucleus. You with me?"

I nod.

"Good. Then start moving along your orbit."

I walk carefully along the first wobbly ring he drew round the nucleus. Suddenly Kristoffer pushes me with both hands, a small, precise push, sending me two steps forward on to the next ring.

"Hey!"

"And there you go – a quantum leap," he says.

I look down at the wavy line beneath my feet.

"One of the electrons that's constantly circling the nucleus does a sort of lane change," he says. "Just a tiny little jump, a minute movement, which creates a discharge of energy. A change in energy levels."

"But why does it switch lanes?"

He throws out his arms. "There are tons of theories but all we really know is that this tiny shift in energy is happening all the time. Constant flux."

"Mysterious," I say.

"Physics is mysterious." Pulling up his sleeve, he holds out his forearm. "Try rubbing this."

I put my hand on his sunburnt skin. The veins stand out

clearly; the hairs are soft and dark. I slowly run my fingers back and forth and it feels like every single nerve ending is buzzing.

"Is that a quantum leap?" I ask, hoping I sound serious and focused.

"No," he says.

"OK … is it an … um … discharge of energy? Like a constant flux or something?"

"No," he says. "It's you rubbing my arm."

He laughs as I pull back my hand and I can't help laughing too. At the same moment, I catch sight of something stirring behind the living-room window – my mum walking past. Maybe Kristoffer sees it too. In any case he checks the time on his phone and hands me the chalk. "I've got to pick up some Jägermeister on the way."

I follow him into the driveway.

"Thanks for dropping off the water blaster," I say.

"You said that already."

"OK, well then, thanks for teaching me something about physics."

"You were a good student."

"I think you're just a good teacher."

He takes a step backwards, narrowing his eyes. "Not about to try and pick a fight with me then, like you usually do?"

"I don't usually fight with you."

"Yeah, you do. But I think you're starting to like me."

"You think so?" I mean to be sarcastic but even I can hear

how I sound – dead serious.

"Yes." He turns, smiling, and says, "See you very soon."

The breakfast table is laid when I enter the kitchen. The wholemeal bread has been sliced and arranged in a curve, and there's a steaming pot of coffee. Mum is in her dressing gown, cutting cheese and sausage by the sink.

"He took his time dropping off that water blaster, didn't he?" says Dad, looking up.

"Nah," is all I say, grabbing a slice of bread and sliding into a chair.

"Aha! Perhaps I'd better keep my nose out of it?" He guffaws.

Cecilie walks into the kitchen in her pyjamas and bunny slippers. "Keep your nose out of what?" she asks, sounding interested, which is unlike her. But maybe it's because Dad's laughing. He doesn't do that much.

"Nothing," I say quickly.

"Oh." Cecilie avoids my eyes as she sits down.

Mum starts nattering about the weather. She says it's clouding over. A few minutes later, it starts to rain, just as Dad predicted. The water pours down the windowpanes and the drainpipe gurgles beneath the open kitchen window.

While I eat, all I can think about is the chalk drawing being washed away.

Tuesday morning starts with a panic attack. Our parents' cars have only just left the driveway when Cecilie begins to hyperventilate until she turns pale. It takes ten minutes of breathing exercises to make her calm down, thirty minutes of snuggling and holding her hand.

I can tell she's afraid of dying today. She's got her death eyes. As though she really thinks her lungs are going to stop absorbing oxygen out of nowhere, that her heart will stop pumping blood.

As we lie on the bed, I run through yesterday's events to work out why she's feeling like this now. We took a break from studying to give her some peace and quiet. We watched two films. Ate dinner. Watched four episodes of a series in her bed. We drank hot chai tea and washed our faces together in the bathroom.

My fingers stroke and stroke and nuzzle and nuzzle. At last she starts to breathe more heavily. She falls asleep. When she wakes, she's feeling better, but doesn't have the energy to revise.

"You hungry?" I ask. "Shall I make us some toast?"

"Toast sounds OK," she says. "And milk."

As I'm waiting for the toaster oven to heat up, a question pops up on my phone:

Wanna come out on the boat?

I stare at Kristoffer's text for several minutes. It's a very impersonal message. Very uninformative. I've no idea, for instance, if he means today or tomorrow, what time we're supposed to set off, or if we'll be the only ones on the boat. There's no emoji to convey his mood or how much he actually wants me to come. I feel like asking all those questions in one long text, but all I can bring myself to answer is:

Why?

Why? Because you want to?

The toaster oven is ready. I put the bread on the rack. Cecilie's bed creaks as though she's turning over or getting out.

When were you thinking?

He answers that it could be now, for example, that we could meet at the harbour in an hour. I imagine the sound of rippling waves and sitting next to Kristoffer while the sun warms our bodies. It's like discovering another very different magnet suddenly attracting me.

"Is the food nearly ready?" Cecilie pops up right behind me. She yawns and stretches.

"In a minute." I put my phone down on the table.

"I feel like I've run a marathon," she says. "My lungs are crazy sore. It's like I've had cramps all night. Can you get cramps in your lungs? Can you get..."

I forget to listen. Opening the kitchen window, I stick my head out and look up at the sky. It's almost cloudless; the heat is clear, not muggy.

"What are you doing?" she says.

"Checking the weather."

"It's not raining, genius."

"Yeah, I know." I'm fussing with the words in my head before I can bring myself to say them. "Kristoffer asked if I want to go out on the boat. So I'm just checking if I need to take sunscreen."

Cecilie turns her back and leaves the kitchen. My heart begins to hammer. I slip my phone into my pocket and follow her into her bedroom.

"I'll be back this afternoon."

No reply. She's lain down on her bed and taken out her laptop.

"You can always call if you need anything?"

Now she just shuts her eyes. I go into my room. My hands are shaking as I tie my long hair into a bun and smear my legs, arms and face with sunscreen.

The phone buzzes.

You coming?

Only now do I realize I never texted Kristoffer back.

I say I'm on my way, toss a water bottle and a tube of sunscreen into a tote, then go and stand in the doorway of Cecilie's room. She's still lying there with her eyes closed, breathing weirdly. I watch her for a while. I'm amazed I don't feel more. That I'm not sorrier for her.

"I'm going now."

She opens her eyes. Stares at me. "Your nose is shiny."

I go into the bathroom and try to wash the sunscreen off my face with a damp cloth, but it's already dried into my skin like a greasy membrane that refuses to dissolve. Cecilie appears in the doorway, watching me as I rub my face.

"Stop it. You'll only give yourself skin cancer." She contemplates me as I check my hair in the mirror from behind and from the side. I adjust the bun a little, sliding in a hairpin.

"I'm still thinking about dropping out," she says. "Maybe that's for the best. I've got such a weird feeling that everything will be over soon anyway. Like I'm not really here."

She's swaying slightly in the door frame.

I get this crazy panicky sensation in my stomach. All I want to do is tuck her up in bed and make her sleep now, now, now.

"Go and lie down," I say. It astonishes me how commanding my voice sounds.

Cecilie looks surprised as well. She obeys immediately. I finish in the bathroom before going back into her room.

"Stop thinking those weird thoughts," I say. "Just sleep."

She pulls the duvet all the way up to her chin. "My poster is falling down."

Leaning over the bed, I press the tattered poster firmly against the wall with a few hard thumps, making the tape reattach. "There we go."

"When are you back?"

"I told you. This afternoon."

"OK." She pulls a face. "Don't forget your life jacket. And don't fall over the side and die."

"I won't. Trust me."

"And don't drown either, Shrimp. If you're going swimming."

I get the urge to suggest we stop with the nicknames once and for all, and I get the urge to say she should put something else above her bed instead of a poster of fucking Winnie-the-Pooh.

"OK," I say, walking backwards out of the door. "No falling, no drowning, no dying."

Kristoffer is waiting at the top of the jetty. He smiles as he catches sight of me.

I'm right here, I remind myself. *Right in the middle of the harbour, in the middle of the crowd. And Cecilie is bound to be asleep already.*

"Is your granddad sailing us?" I ask as we walk down the jetty.

"They let me take the boat out of the harbour by myself. Not too far, where there's a bit of a breeze."

"OK, but then we should put our life jackets on, shouldn't we?"

"If you want to look like an idiot because you're in water three metres deep," he says, "then sure – be my guest."

"But you've got … a driving licence for it?"

He laughs. "A skipper's licence. Don't you trust me?

My dad taught me to drive a boat. You've got to be able to when you live in Greenland."

We leave the harbour with the engine droning beneath us. Barely a hundred metres from the jetty, we start to chug slowly along the coast until we reach some big, colourful warehouses surrounded by dark green forest. Pine needles that have drifted out from the shoreline are floating in the water around us. We sit down at the back of the boat where a small, mouldering set of steps leads down to the sea. Submerging our feet in the water, we relax in the falling shadow of the wheelhouse. I regret being so thorough with the sunscreen.

As I dip my toes, my gaze falls on the black letters winding up the stern. I lean forward slightly so I can read the whole name.

"*Carpe Diem*?" I say. "No, no, no. That doesn't suit an old boat like this at all. Plus it's not even a name! It should be called *Susan*. Or *Ulla-Magrethe*."

Kristoffer laughs.

I say, "Anyway, *Carpe Diem* is just so unoriginal. All that inspirational-quote bullshit makes me sick. Seriously, who actually gets *more* enthusiastic about life after hearing that stuff?"

"If you only had one day left on earth, what would you

do?" he asks, apparently having not heard a word of what I've just said.

"I don't know." I can't even be bothered to think about such a silly, hypothetical question.

"Come on," he says. "We could fall into the water and drown. Or you could die of a heart defect nobody knew was there. Have you used your last day well?"

"With *you*?"

"OK, OK." He gets to his feet, starts walking round the wheelhouse. I stay where I am. Eventually he's out of sight. I move my legs into the sunshine and check my phone.

No messages. I text Cecilie a heart, which she'll see when she wakes up.

"Here you go." He's back, prodding my shoulder with an ice-cold bottle of beer, which I accept, before he sits down next to me.

"Is it OK to drink when you're steering a boat?"

"It's fine."

I let him help me open the bottle. It fizzes over, the foam dripping down my hand in a thick stripe. I lick it off. The taste of salt, sunscreen and bitter hops fills my mouth.

"So you *can* drink beer," he says.

"Why wouldn't I be able to?"

"I just never see you at parties." He smiles.

"You saw me drinking schnapps last week," I say. "And maybe I just don't go to the same places you do. I've had quite meaningful conversations with people at parties, actually. You're probably just standing at the bar. Or thrashing around on the dance floor."

"I don't dance," Kristoffer says. "But I do like hanging out at the bar, sure."

"With your charming friends?"

He turns his face to mine. I'm not all that crazy about the way he's looking at me.

"Why do you act so hard all the time?" He sounds almost hurt.

"It's not an act. It's the way I am."

"No, it's not. You always believed the best in other people. When I knew you, you never said a bad word about anyone. You cried if someone teased you – you got really sad."

"I was ten when you left," I say. "I've got a bit older and wiser since then."

He sips his beer.

"I think about you and Cecilie a lot, actually – the way you used to be. And not just you two but your whole family. Your mum always home early, baking rolls. Your dad building swing sets and playhouses for you."

Sometimes I almost forget, but he's right: there was a time when our family was the place I felt safest of all.

"People remember stuff through rose-tinted glasses, don't you think?" I ask. "They deceive themselves somehow?"

"Maybe. People do change, of course." He picks up one of the bottle caps from the deck, flicks it into the air, catches it. "Everything changes."

"Like with quantum leaps?"

He smiles. "Like with quantum leaps."

"But what if you're addicted to safety?" I ask. "If you don't like change but you also don't like the way things are now?" I'm not sure if I'm thinking of Cecilie or myself as I ask the question.

"Then you've got a problem." Kristoffer looks so flippant as he says it that I can't help giving his shoulder a pat.

"So I guess you're not a safety addict yourself?"

"I've never been like that."

He draws up his legs, stretches his arms and rests them on his knees, gazing out across the water. That's how I remember him as a child: sitting on the roof of the playhouse in his garden, spying on Cecilie and me over the hedge.

I say, "*All* children are addicted to safety."

"Not me. I've never had the solid base you have. I think it makes you a bit less likely to seek security."

"You did have that until your parents split up, though?"

"Nah. My dad was depressed half the time. That was one of the reasons we moved to Greenland. He missed his family." He's fiddling with the beer bottle, scratching at the label. "And the landscape."

"Did it get better in Nuuk?"

"It went OK the first three years. Until I was … fifteen maybe. Then he went into this massive spiral. He was on medication but in the end he was just like some zombie down in his black cave, and he didn't give a shit about anything. He didn't even try. Then Mum left him. She said I should come and live with her." He glances down a moment before raising his head. "It wasn't exactly fun living with someone who could barely bring himself to take a shower."

"You didn't find it hard to leave him?"

I imagine Kristoffer's dad all alone in a small dark house on the tip of an ice floe.

"No," he says. "It felt like he was the one leaving us." Something hard appears in his voice. "And it was a good thing Mum left him. She's happy now."

I wonder how his father is doing but I don't need to ask. Kristoffer starts to tell me of his own accord. "Last time I visited he said he's started doing this group therapy thing for men. He's obviously got some shit from childhood that's still on his mind. I don't know what it is. But…"

He flicks the bottle cap in the air again but this time he can't catch it before it drops into the water.

"In a way I think he needed that kick to get going. Otherwise I reckon we'd be in the same place. Maybe even somewhere worse. Mum had to leave him. It was either that or be dragged down herself. She says so too."

"Ouch," I say because it's the first thing that comes to mind.

He shrugs. "Not many people know that's why they split up. People have this automatic reaction because he's from Greenland. It's so obvious what they're thinking: Greenlandic men are all drunk, depressed or suicidal – or all three."

The water gurgles behind the boat. My toes are getting cold. I pull them out.

"I'm glad you told me," I say. "I think maybe I understand you a bit better now."

"Yeah, well, I'm probably kind of difficult to understand." He plants his arms behind him and leans back, looking at me. "Unlike you. One look at you and it's obvious what you're thinking."

"What am I thinking right now then?"

"Right now?" His eyes run slowly up and down me. "You're thinking … what is he up to, that creepy douche bag? Spilling all his childhood traumas, trying to get some sympathy."

"That's not even funny," I say. "And it's not true anyway."

He smiles at me. Somehow it's a shy smile.

I say, "But I still don't know why you invited me out here."

"Don't you?"

"No."

"And you can't take a guess?"

"No," I say.

He takes a sip of his beer, then another and another. "For one thing, I think you're beautiful."

I can think of nothing to say except, "And the other thing?"

He takes his time answering. "It's pretty simple, actually. I want to make you happy."

"Why?" Kind of a conceited question, I guess. But I need to know the answer.

"It's just this weird mechanism that got installed in me when I moved back. I saw you around school and then…" He puts on a robotic voice. "*Make. Astrid. Happy.*"

"Because I was looking sad?!"

"I'm just telling you what it feels like." He moves a little, a tiny shuffle of the body, lessening the distance between us. "I keep asking myself the whole time: how can I make Astrid smile? Any time I come up with something that might be the answer, I want to do it."

His hand is next to mine. His face is right up close.

And I think I should kiss him.

That the moment is now.

But my heart is hammering way too hard for me to do any such thing.

He looks down at our hands, side by side on the deck, then puts his big hand on top of mine, interlacing our fingers. I look at them too now, the fingers.

There's a throbbing in my face.

In my lips.

In my groin.

My heart is pumping blood to every single part of my body, parts I never really thought were alive. And then I feel a warmth behind my eyes, which makes it impossible to remove my gaze from our hands. I didn't know it was possible to feel this way and it hurts. It hurts like hell because you're not allowed to be that happy.

"Would you rather we just … stay friends?" he asks.

I shake my head.

He's still looking at me, waiting. It's my turn to speak. I want to and I don't want to. Finally I blurt it out: "I'm scared."

He's quiet for a long time. So long that for a minute I start to wonder if I even said the words out loud, or if he's struggling not to laugh at me. Then he gives my fingers a squeeze.

"What are you scared of?"

My eyes are still fixed on our hands and I have to swallow several times to be sure my voice won't break. "Of being this happy right now."

He doesn't take his eyes off me.

It's rare for someone other than Cecilie to look at me that way. So very incredibly close. Actually, I don't remember it ever happening before. He can see all the imperfections in my face. Every single blemish, every single pore. And I should be terrified – I'm full of flaws.

He says, "It's OK to be happy."

Then he kisses me.

It's not a long kiss. Only our lips greeting each other for a second before he pulls away and smiles, not at me, but almost to himself. Then he shuffles even closer, putting his arm round me. Tilting his head and kissing my shoulder.

I start to shake. My whole body is seized with cold and nausea, as though he's just given me the flu.

"You're shivering," he says. "Are you cold?"

As I cycle home slowly from the harbour, I'm someone else. It's not me pushing the pedals around, it's a strange girl – softer, more cautious, happier, as though it's the first time in her life she's sat on a bike. But when I reach our house, I turn back into myself. Dad's car is already in the driveway and it's only half past four. He's not normally home this early. And the door to the utility room is rattling open in a way it never usually does because Mum hates the draught.

"What exactly do you want me to do?"

"It's not like I've got a manual for this stuff, do I?"

The voices are coming from the kitchen. Mum sounds tired. "Well, can you at least call and talk to them? There must be some sort of procedure."

"A travel company is a business, not some kind of charity. They couldn't care less; they just want to see the doctor's note. We can talk about it once you've been to the GP with her."

"So now it's up to me to do everything by myself again?"

I walk through the door. Mum is sitting on the edge of a chair. She's got her fingers pressed against her temples, as though trying to equalize an enormous pressure. Dad's just standing in front of her, glaring and shifting his weight from one foot to the other.

Why can he never see that he only has to give her a hug? That that's what she needs right now – nothing else. Maybe you run out of hugs at some point in a marriage. Maybe that's what's happened. So you just stand there and glare at each other, not knowing how to get beyond that.

"Astrid!" Mum drops her hands at the sight of me. "Where have you been all day long? I thought you two were going to study together?"

The knot in my stomach tightens again. "What's wrong?"

She says, "Cecilie wants to cancel all her exams."

It's like being hit by a wave that knocks you off your feet and cuts off your oxygen supply for several seconds.

"She wants to do the make-up exams in August instead. Cecilie says you've talked about it more than once?"

As Mum talks, Dad is staring at me. It feels like his eyes are saying what his mouth isn't: *I thought we had a deal, Astrid? I thought we were going to get Cecilie through this?*

I head down the corridor and stop outside Cecilie's door. My knuckles tap the wood and I stare at my hand, at the thin purple veins twisting underneath the skin. It's the same hand as always but suddenly I can see the hand could have acted differently.

For a moment, I consider going back down the corridor and out through the kitchen, simply leaving the house. Then I open the door, and now everything feels like it usually does; everything's behaving as usual. My sister is sitting up in bed, and I go straight to her side and take her hand in mine.

"Mum and Dad are flipping out." She's been crying. She's only just stopped. There are still channels of tears on her pale face. "I told them I've been thinking about it for ages, that I want to take the make-up exams in August instead. So now we have to move the summer holiday to July, and it's difficult, and Dad is angry." She shuts her eyes for a long moment before reopening them. "I've got to go to the doctor with Mum on Monday and get a note."

"But … why do you want to sit the exams later?"

"Because I'm going through a bad patch."

I think: *But what if your bad patch lasts for months? What if you're not ready by August? What if your bad patch isn't a patch but the rest of your life?*

"Will they let you?" I swallow. "Just like that?"

"Yes, if we get a doctor's note. And luckily they know my history," she says. "Mum's called and made an appointment with the student counsellor on Monday, right after the doctor's. Going to see Jacob is just … a formality." She snivels. "Will you come?"

"Of course."

"Dad thinks it's silly." Cecilie blinks her eyes rapidly but the tears are coming anyway. "Do you think it's stupid too?"

Everything is collapsing in my head, like a building I was naïve enough to think I could walk into alone. If the holiday in Crete is moved to July, there's a risk it will clash with my interrailing trip with Jonas. And what happens if Cecilie doesn't take the exams till August? Will she spend the whole summer holiday studying? Will I be studying with her?

"It's not stupid," I finally manage to say. "It'll be fine."

"You think so?"

"Yeah. Of course."

Suddenly she stares at me as though she's noticed a peculiar spot on my face. "You look happy."

My heart begins to hammer, hard and irregular, at the thought of my afternoon. "Do I?"

"You kissed, didn't you? You and Kristoffer?"

"Um … yes."

"Once?"

I can't even begin to think about counting all the kisses. "I haven't forgotten what you said about him. That he's random with girls. But it all seemed really, well … genuine."

"OK."

She bites a nail as though my answer has made her nervous.

I'm on the verge of asking her if she thinks Kristoffer is the type of guy to lie about wanting to make me happy. If she thinks that's something he says to every new girl whose pants he's trying to get into.

But I don't want to hear her answer right now.

I want to be happy.

"Are you in love with him?" she asks as she sits there, staring at me and chewing her nails.

"No," I say, with a snorting laugh that comes out of nowhere.

"Are you seeing him again?"

"Mm ... yeah. On Friday. His place."

She starts breathing more deeply. It sounds like there's something sitting on her ribcage that she's trying to lift off with the aid of her lungs alone.

"Shall I open the window?" I ask, already on my feet.

She shakes her head.

"Maybe you just need to be tucked in properly?" I suggest.

I watch myself as if from outside as I arrange the duvet more tightly, tucking it firmly round her body, the way she likes it – the sensation of being in a warm, safe cocoon.

"Sorry," she says as she lies there with only her face peeping out. "It's not that I don't want to hear about it. Just not right now."

"Of course."

"It's just been a shitty day. Sorry."

"Stop apologizing."

It was my big sister who was the first one of us to climb trees, the first to ride a bike with no hands. She should have been the first one to get a boyfriend, to finish high school, to pave the way. That's how it is with big sisters: they're supposed to do things you're not ready for yet; they're supposed to be wise and strong; and you're supposed to look up to them, to be a bit jealous of them in secret.

I'm sure Cecilie thinks about how things should stand between us.

That I should be the little sister.

That she should be the big sister.

And I wish I was able to tell her that it doesn't matter. That it's totally beside the point. That I love her exactly as she is.

I can hear her now, crying on the other side of the wall. Not the crying that means she wants Mum or me to hear. The kind you try to stifle in a pillow.

I wish I was better at being a big sister to my big sister.

On my way to Kristoffer's place on Friday afternoon it all starts to feel a bit unreal. I'm having trouble making space for anything in my head besides my parents' disappointed faces and Cecilie, who has curled up into a little ball that rolls in and out of bed, eating meals and watching TV series.

The boat, the kissing: it all seems like a childish dream.

But then he answers the door and it feels like a law of nature that we should kiss right there and then, just by the door. Afterwards we hug. We just stand there holding each other for what feels like ages.

"I wasn't sure you'd come," he says, his mouth against my hair.

"What?" I can't help laughing.

"You play it so cool via text." He lets me go. Pulls a funny face. "I feel like a drooling puppy."

First we sit for a while in their garden, a small square of grass with a few pieces of lawn furniture. Afterwards we go upstairs.

It's not long before we're lying on the bed.

His mouth is warm and tastes nice. My top slides up and he draws a circle round my navel with his finger. I hold my breath. Then I let my fingers wander up underneath his T-shirt, exploring the contours of his muscles, the silky-soft hair on the lowest part of his stomach.

He smiles, watching me.

I have no idea what he's thinking.

Maybe he feels like I'm dragging my feet. Maybe he's disappointed I haven't thrown off my sweater and straddled him, that I haven't grabbed his dick and put it in my mouth. I brush the cold metal buckle with the very tips of my fingers, getting closer to the bulge. A jolt runs through his body.

"I don't have any condoms." His voice is hoarse; he clears his throat. "I know that's dumb."

"OK, but … I'm not on the pill."

"I didn't mean—" he says. "I was just trying to manage your expectations." He smiles. "Lower them."

"Oh."

I'm relieved this can't end in sex, but I try to look neutral. Like a girl who wouldn't sleep with anybody anyway until she's dated them for a couple of weeks.

We lie there, stroking each other for a while, without

saying a word. His eyes are slightly foggy. Every so often he squints them hard, whenever I touch a particular place on his body – the soft skin close to his armpit.

"I've only ever done it before when I was drunk, actually," he says. "In a way I'm kind of a sober virgin, I guess. To be honest, I don't know how it works when you're not drunk. Maybe my dick needs vodka to function?"

This is probably the moment I should laugh and tell him I'm a virgin myself, that the number of experiences I've had of being half naked with a guy can be counted on one finger and are roughly a year old.

"Did I kill the mood?" he asks when I say nothing.

"A little."

"Thought so."

I swallow. I want to share something of myself. "I'm glad you invited me out on the boat."

"Are you?"

He sounds so surprised, I'm almost offended. "Yes. Why shouldn't I be?"

"When I got back last summer, you stared daggers at me every time I even said hello."

"I don't think that's quite true." I shift slightly, widening the gap between our faces.

"I mean, it would have been normal to chat a bit when we bumped into each other. Like, 'Hey, Kristoffer, welcome back. How've you been getting on?'"

"But you were always going round with those too-cool-for-school idiots. I don't think I ever saw you in the hall alone."

"Hey. Be nice about my friends." He pinches my earlobe. "And remember there's always something behind the too-cool-for-school-ness. Like there's always something behind the nerdiness and the hardness and the sweetness."

"I know everybody's hiding something behind the façade," I say.

"Do you?" He takes a lock of my hair, slowly lifting it up.

"Yes." I pull my hair back. "So no need for a lecture in basic psychology, thank you."

He bites his bottom lip crookedly, an expression that's half uncertain, half apologetic. "Is Cecilie doing any better, by the way?"

This is the only question Jonas can think to ask about my sister too. This question, which is the most logical and makes me the most frustrated. As though she's got a cold and should be getting over it.

"Actually, she's decided to do the make-up exams in August instead." My throat tightens. "To take the pressure off."

He takes my hand and squeezes it. "You're upset about it?"

"Nah." I force a smile. "It just sucks she'll have to spend her summer holiday revising."

The student counsellor's office is right next to the secretaries' area. Mum goes in to tell them we've arrived. Cecilie is clenching my fingers. We've been holding hands the whole way down, including in the doctor's waiting room and in the car, while Mum put talk radio on and checked us in the rear-view mirror every other second.

Now we're standing in the hallway, staring at all the students gathered in the Bathtub. There's a faint hum from the small groups chatting at the tables. The odd few students and teachers cross paths in the hallways, pacing swiftly. I can feel it physically in my stomach – the thrum of pre-exam nerves and post-exam excitement.

In four days it will be my turn.

"Jacob's going to be so disappointed in me," says Cecilie.

Giving her hand a squeeze, I say, "He'll get it."

In addition to the meetings our parents have been summoned to because of her absences, my sister has attended regular 'welfare check-ins' of her own over the years, with the student counsellor. Jacob is one of the only adults at the school Cecilie actually likes. One of the only ones she feels has tried to understand what she's grappling with. It was his job to keep all Cecilie's teachers in the loop about her 'psychological challenges' and ask them to take her situation into account as much as possible.

I often wonder what the teachers really think about a student like my sister. If they want to get her through, or if they reckon she's too weak and should give up.

I sit down on a bench outside school and wait while Mum and Cecilie go inside for the meeting. The sun is blazing and I roll up the sleeves of my T-shirt, take out my phone and text Jonas to say I'm hanging out at school for the next half-hour if he wants to join me. He lives right next door so he could be here in two minutes if he felt like it.

Sorry, just got into the bath.

He sends a picture of his bare legs slung over the edge of a cracked bathtub, plus a bottle of chocolate milk.

OK, well, I'll just sit here by myself then...

Let me know if you want more pictures, he writes, without commenting on my solitude.

I'm pretty sure me and Jonas won't be best friends when we start second year after the summer. I haven't told him about Cecilie cancelling her exams yet and he hasn't asked. I haven't told him who I'm seeing either. All in all, there's this weird new rift between us and I don't know how I'm going to get across.

I call Kristoffer. He picks up straight away. There's a pleasant bubbly sensation in my belly. I might not have Jonas any more but I have Kristoffer instead. He's there for me. Always. Every time.

"Do you want me to come down there?" he asks.

My phone pings and I imagine it's Jonas changing his mind, saying he's going to join me after all.

"It's fine," I say.

"I'm just in the garden, trying to study, but I'd really like to be distracted," he says. "And you sound sad."

"It feels weird she's not going to graduate like the rest of you," I say. "Just ... wrong."

"Are you sure you don't want me to come down?"

At that moment, I catch sight of Caroline. She's walking towards me in that tentative, rodenty way. When we lock eyes, she looks away but I raise my arm and wave so vehemently she can't ignore me. Now she heads in my direction.

"Maybe we can see each other tomorrow," I say. "Your place?"

"Aren't I going to see the inside of your house soon?"

"At some point," I say.

He's silent a moment. "I feel like maybe I think about you too much. It's a bit dangerous."

"Why is it dangerous?"

"Because I'm still not sure you like me."

"You're silly."

We say goodbye and I end the call just as Caroline comes to a halt in front of me.

"Hi," she says. "You got an exam today?"

"No, I'm waiting for Mum and Cecilie. They're talking to Jacob."

"Oh," is all she says.

I'm genuinely surprised she doesn't seem to care what Cecilie is doing in the student counsellor's office.

"They'll be out in a minute. Maybe you could stick around and say hello?"

"I've got German in half an hour." She glances at her watch, looks away. "I'd better get inside."

She doesn't ask me to say hello to Cecilie for her – she just starts walking off. I feel like running after her and asking what kind of shitty friend she is. If she really has no intention of being there for Cecilie when she's at rock bottom. But maybe I was right the whole time. Maybe they're just the kind of friends who only hang out because everyone else is already in a group.

When I look at my phone, it's not Jonas who texted but Veronica.

Hi, Astrid. What time is your exam on Friday? I'll come and root for you :)

Cecilie has been approved to take the make-up exams by the doctor and the student counsellor. The only thing left is to change the tickets with the travel company. Mum seems relieved that evening. Dad goes on a long run. After I've said goodnight to Cecilie and started getting ready for bed, Mum comes into my room and shuts the door behind her.

"There's something we need to talk about. It's to do with the summer holiday," she says, letting her eyes flit round my room as though astonished by the sight. No Winnie-the-Pooh posters or stuffed animals, only clothes and books and bags.

"What?" I flop down on the bed.

"As you know, we need to move the holiday. And since August is no longer a possibility, it looks like it will fit your dad's work schedule best if we set off on Saturday the eighteenth of July." She gives a small, unhappy smile.

"I *know* that clashes with your trip with Jonas. Is there any way you could move it?"

"Well, we've already bought interrail passes. The only days we can travel are in July."

"But couldn't you go *before* the eighteenth?"

"Jonas is going to Sweden with his mum and his brothers," I say. "They always do that in the first two weeks of July."

"OK." Mum rubs her eyes with her hand. "Of course you should go with Jonas. You've both been looking forward to that trip for so long. Dad and I understand that. We'll just have to do without you."

But I can tell from her face that it will be a catastrophe, of course. No way the three of them could stand each other for a whole week without their connecting link.

"I can go with you guys, I guess," I say after a deep in-breath.

She tries to protest but the words come out of her mouth in small drowned phrases even she can't manage to save. "No … sweetheart … it's important to you … you've got to … Jonas will be so…"

"I mean it," I say. "It's OK. Really."

"Are you sure?" She looks so tired. Like someone kept up all night by an unreasonable, shrieking infant.

"Yeah," I say. "I'd rather go on holiday with you guys."

She gives me a hug. For a moment, I'm afraid she's going to cry.

"Thank you," she says.

Social studies has got me all flushed and sticky. Coming out of the exam room, I avoid hugs from Jonas and Veronica by pointing in disgust at the sweat stains that have blossomed on my top. They both did theirs yesterday but I didn't go and see them, excusing myself by saying I needed to study.

"Did it go all right?" Jonas is standing closer to Veronica than he normally stands to anybody. My best friend likes to say he has a problem with personal space.

"I don't know."

"What did you get?" asks Veronica.

"Development aid."

When I'm called in two minutes later, our teacher is already smiling in the doorway, and I haven't even sat down before the examiner tells me I've got a good handle on the material, that my explanation was clear and precise, and that I can leave for the summer with the highest possible mark, a twelve. Jonas and Veronica cheer and somehow it seems taken as read that we'll go down to the harbour to celebrate, now the three of us are done.

Half an hour later, we're slurping cappuccinos and eating blueberry muffins. Jonas burps so loudly that Veronica whacks him on the back and says, "Howdy, cowboy!"

And, yeah, I can see it: they might actually be pretty cute together.

"Nothing but holiday now," says Jonas. "Man, it's awesome! All that freedom!"

"*Yeeaaaah!*" says Veronica, glancing sidelong at me. "Holiday!"

I haven't spoken to either of them about the interrail trip since my awkward meet-up at the café with Jonas. Maybe they're both waiting for me to bring it up, or maybe they've already made plans behind my back.

"Yeah, holiday, yay," I say.

Jonas slaps me on the shoulder. "Is something wrong?"

"Nah. The Crete holiday just got moved to the middle of July, and I know we said we were supposed to be travelling then, but I guess you two will just have to go by yourselves instead." I pull the corners of my mouth all the way down, until I can feel the tension in my temples. "See! It turned out just like you predicted!"

They both stare at me without a word. The silence feels embarrassing.

"I need to pee." Veronica sets down her cup and rises. Then she clacks calmly down the promenade in her purple Crocs. We watch her go without a word, until she's turning the corner towards the toilets.

"Why does the holiday have to be moved?" Jonas asks at last.

"Because Cecilie is taking the make-up exams in August. In every subject."

He falls silent again. Inside I'm hoping the silence is covering his embarrassment at not asking me how things are going at home.

"You don't think this is the best thing for her?" he says.

"Do you think so?"

"OK, it's shit, of course. But if you take a broader perspective, she's probably still going to graduate. And it's not like she's dying, is it?"

Death is basically Jonas's trump card. It's pretty difficult to argue with that.

"Don't people also say that it's time people started thinking of mental illness like a broken leg?" he continues. "It's not taboo any more, is it?"

I've never understood the urge to make that comparison.

People with broken legs have a broken leg.

People with anxiety have a black hood pulled down over their head.

"No, she's not dying," I say. "That's true."

"I still don't understand why nobody's tried giving her medication." His voice is low, almost a murmur. "If she's really doing as crappily as you say."

For a brief moment, I consider pelting him with all the pent-up words in my head.

My dad is against medication and thinks anxiety is something that needs to be fought with willpower. Mum says Cecilie should make up her own mind, while the doctor recommends medication and therapy, but how do you force a nineteen-year-old to do anything she doesn't want to do? Anyway, my dad has one idea about what demands they can make on my sister and my mum has a completely different one. They argue about it all the time and I'm afraid they don't love each other any more. I'm afraid they stopped being on the same team a long time ago.

I could start explaining all that but I just don't have it in me.

The seagulls are hopping closer. Spreading their wings backwards, their eyes fixed on our cake crumbs, they're screaming hoarsely.

"Are you absolutely sure you want to just drop out of our trip?" Jonas asks. "Shouldn't they understand it's more important to you to travel with us than with them? You're seventeen."

"I need to go with them. They can't get along by themselves otherwise."

"But is that your problem?" he asks. "Do you have to be the martyr in all this?"

I shoot him a look, so he's in no doubt he needs to shut up.

He clears his throat. "Have you told your parents what

you got?"

"Not yet."

I take out my phone. Two texts. One from my mum, asking how it went. One from Kristoffer, asking the same thing but with more words. Cecilie hasn't texted. I promised her I would. I send a 12 to all of them. Nothing else.

Kristoffer responds straight away:

Social studies queen! Happy holiday!

I start typing an answer.

"Are you texting Cecilie?" Jonas sounds like someone from Alcoholics Anonymous who's just caught a whiff of vodka on my breath.

"No," I say. "If you really want to know, I'm texting Kristoffer."

"Ex-neighbour Kristoffer?" His eyes go wide. "There's a lot of stuff happening in your life, huh?"

I shrug. "We've only seen each other a couple of times."

"Good for you." He gives me an odd little smile. "I mean it. If you're happy, that's awesome."

I think: *Can you really not tell how I'm doing? Can you not see that it's impossible for me to swan around all happy while my sister's life is stuck on repeat?*

When Veronica comes back, she settles down right next to Jonas.

We say no more about interrailing that afternoon.

Our summer holiday falls into place the next day. The tickets have been changed, so we're setting off in mid-July. This means Cecilie has nearly two weeks to study before she takes her first make-up exam. I've almost come to terms with the situation. The interrail trip with Jonas wouldn't be the same anyway with Veronica in tow. And maybe we really will relax by the pool, the four of us – maybe that's exactly what we need.

Everything will be better now, I tell myself.

Everything will calm down.

But reality doesn't work like that.

Cecilie says she had a dream the plane crashed, that we all burned like living torches in the dark before falling into the sea and dying. And now she's scared of going to sleep – she's afraid of dreaming the same dream.

"You've got to stop dwelling on stuff like that," I say. "Think how many planes take off every day, and everything's fine."

But you can't argue with anxiety. She keeps talking about it and she keeps dreaming about it.

Then Mum is in the kitchen telling my sister that if she's still afraid of flying when it's time to leave she'll stay home with her and Dad and I can go on holiday by ourselves. I go into the garden, hide behind sunglasses and earbuds, playing music. Moments later, Mum comes out and sits down next to me, reassuring me that of course all four of us will go. The stuff about staying at home is just her way of reassuring Cecilie so she doesn't feel pressured and stops obsessing all the time.

It makes sense.

You'd think it would help.

But after their talk, it seems like my sister is worse than ever. She cries a lot. Not quiet, private crying in her room, but snot and tears and sobs that spill into the kitchen, into the hall, everywhere she drags herself around in joggers.

I think constantly of the future as small grey fields we need to cross, to get through. It's still June, so maybe Cecilie will feel better once exams are over and she's not perpetually being reminded that she won't graduate with everyone else. In three weeks we're going to Crete, and afterwards she can take the make-up exams and move on with her life.

I hope that's how it will be.

I can almost convince myself it will.

But then I hear my parents arguing in the living room on Saturday night. Mum says she wants Cecilie to go back to the doctor for referral to a psychiatrist. Dad says there's no point and that she's not so far gone she's a suicide risk.

"What kind of argument is that?" Mum's voice rises after his use of the word 'suicide'. "And how do you even know?"

I regret eavesdropping. I really don't want to stand here and listen to them talk that way, and now it feels like something cold has clenched my heart.

"She's apathetic," he says. "Anybody can see that."

"Yes, and that's precisely why I want her evaluated by a psychiatrist. What if there's something else wrong? What if it's not *just* anxiety?"

"What else would it be?"

"You know what? You're not the one trying to find out what's going on with our daughter. It's *me*! And she seems depressed!"

"Yes, of course." He gives a harsh snort. "Surely that can't come as a surprise? Depression is a natural reaction when your life is stagnating."

I don't want to hear any more. I go into my room and bury my head in the pillow, muffling my tears so that no one will hear.

When I wake up the next morning, I slip past Cecilie's door even though I can hear her calling. I take a long walk round the streets. Settling on the kerb, I observe people's morning rituals: dog-walkers, runners hurtling along in neon, cars being filled with kids and backed out of driveways.

I get a text from Kristoffer asking if I want to come over that evening.

Aren't you supposed to be revising for history?

It's his last exam, the most important; the grade he gets in it will be written on his hat – the red-and-white hat with a black peak, which every student gets to wear if they pass. He should be stressed and manic but he's not. He's done well in the other exams, so why wouldn't he do well in this one? That's just the way he thinks. To him, everything seems so easy.

Yeah, but I'd rather see you :)

OK, then I'll come over.

That afternoon I watch a film with Cecilie in her room, massaging her scalp in silence. Her hair is greasy. When she falls asleep around five, I go wash my fingers thoroughly with soap and water before I head into the kitchen where Mum is busy cooking.

In the moment before she notices me I contemplate her. Our mother has lost weight this year; there are streaks of grey in her hair. If you're not making direct eye contact with her, if she's not moving her face to oblige someone else, the skin around her mouth and eyes looks as slack and pale as overproofed dough.

"Mum?"

She looks up.

"I'm going over to Kristoffer's in a bit."

"Wouldn't you like to invite him here instead?" She gestures towards the lasagne she's making. "We've got enough food. Then we could also meet him properly?"

I feel like saying I'm not inviting anyone to our house the way things are right now. Does she really think it would be nice to have a witness here while we crumble?

"Kristoffer already told Ellen I'm joining them for dinner," I say. "She's cooking for us."

"OK." Mum turns on the tap, rinsing the sink clean.

I wonder if she would have the 'safe-sex talk' with me if she had a little more energy. It must have occurred to her by now that Kristoffer and I might decide to sleep together or might already have done so. The thought makes me feel weird. I'm relieved she hasn't managed to talk to me about it, but I'm also strangely disappointed.

"I'm going now." I start backing towards the utility-room door.

"Hang on a minute." She pulls me into a hug that lasts too long and feels like it has nothing to do with me. "I just think it's a bit tough on Cecilie that you're not around so much any more. You're so good together. You have such a special bond." Finally she lets go. "I'd just be so sad if you two lost that."

I can't concentrate on our bodies, mine or Kristoffer's. I'm nothing but a head. At last I have to push him away and sit up.

He lies there, watching me.

Again I have no clue what he's thinking and it stresses me out.

"I think maybe I'm coming down with something," I say, which is silly but instantly he reaches out a hand and rests it against my cheek.

"You are a bit warm actually…"

And suddenly I do feel like that – sick, as though a fever's on the way. I realize I've got a stomachache. My skin is clammy.

He's scrutinizing my face. "Your eyes are kind of shiny too…"

And then he smiles because he thinks there's nothing

wrong behind them but I can sense that everything is wrong, that everything about my life feels so insanely difficult. As though people are tugging at me from all sides and I can't be in any of those places. I'm just torn into more and more pieces.

He frowns. "There's nothing wrong, is there?"

"It's just Cecilie." I force myself to sound calm. "She's going through another bad patch."

"I thought things had calmed down after the holiday stuff got sorted?"

"Not really."

"Come here," he says. "Come lie next to me."

We stay like that for ages. He strokes the bridge of my nose until I shut my eyes. Mum used to do the same thing when I was little and couldn't fall asleep. Now something starts to burn behind my eyelids.

"Can I say something?" he asks. "Something that might sound a little harsh, but it's not meant that way."

I know what he wants to say.

I don't want to hear it.

But he says it anyway, without waiting for an answer: "Only Cecilie can save Cecilie."

Kristoffer's dad had to save himself. Kristoffer knows exactly what mental illness can do to a person and I can't contradict him. But my stomach clenches even harder. His words leave something in me that hurts, that feels wrong.

I sit up again.

He's still lying down.

"Think I need to go home."

A few houses down the road, Ellen catches up with me. She comes jogging up, slinging a cardigan round her.

"Astrid! Wait!" She's panting. "You can't go home by yourself at this time of night."

"It's fine."

"I should have taught Kristoffer that you don't let a girl walk home alone this late," she says.

I'm about to protest this doubly sexist statement when she puts her arm through mine, as though we're two friends. And suddenly I get the strong feeling that she caught up with me for an entirely different reason than the dark and the time.

"You're always welcome to sleep over," she says.

"Thanks. It just wasn't convenient today."

We continue in silence for a while.

"I understand from Kristoffer that Cecilie has postponed her exams?"

It's hard for me to answer. The stillness around us is too great; the stars are too far up. I don't want to cry.

"Has Kristoffer ever told you about his father?" she asks.

"Mm."

She gives my arm a squeeze. "I know what it's like.

I know what a burden it puts on families. I've been there. Tell your mum I'm always here to talk if she needs to. There are all sorts of courses, you know? For relatives. You can learn the best ways to tackle that sort of thing."

I pick up the pace. What I really want to ask is why she left her husband then, if there are these courses that fix everything? Why did she abandon him in Greenland all alone in the middle of a deep depression?

Do you really have to leave the people you love to force them to save themselves?

"Or I could come over to your place one evening," she continues. "We could do a group meditation. I can teach you some relaxation techniques so you can all—"

I tear my arm away. "Does Kristoffer tell you *everything* I tell him?"

She looks embarrassed. "Of course not."

My heart is pounding. It's the first time I've spoken to an adult like that. Now I'm on the verge of tears again.

"I'm sorry if I expressed myself poorly," she says quietly. "I'm sure you're the best sister in the world."

I have no idea whether Ellen told Kristoffer about our conversation, but the mere thought of ever seeing her again makes me embarrassed. I'm sure she thinks all sorts of terrible stuff about our family now. That she – like Jonas – believes we ought to pull ourselves together.

After all, nobody's died.

Kristoffer's last exam is three days before the graduation celebration. That morning I want to go over there, and I don't want to. I really can't make up my mind. Eventually I'm so desperate I text Jonas and ask what he would do in my shoes.

He calls me.

"Do you like him or what?" Jonas sounds irritated, as though I've disturbed him in the middle of something, but frankly he didn't have to call if it was really that inconvenient.

"I mean, it's complicated." I still can't make myself tell him about the conversation with Ellen, so I just rephrase the same sentence. "It's not that simple."

"Yes, it is! Pull yourself together."

It's good advice. I decide to go down to school. As I'm getting ready, Cecilie comes trudging up and stands in the doorway.

"What are you doing?" she asks.

"Going to see Kristoffer get his graduation cap."

"Oh … OK." She leans against the frame, almost collapsing.

I can't bear to look at her so I start rummaging in my chest of drawers for a lipgloss. There's a strange stillness in the room. As I press my lips together in front of the mirror, distributing the colour, they make a much-too-loud kissing noise.

"Are you remembering to use condoms?"

"*What?!*"

Our eyes meet in the mirror. I can see my face turning red, while she stands absolutely motionless by the door.

"Are you using condoms?" she repeats.

I know instantly that what I do or don't do with Kristoffer is definitely not something I want to share with my sister. I don't know why, since we share everything else, but suddenly I feel an almost physical distaste at her question.

"If you get chlamydia, you can have a pelvic infection without realizing and end up sterile. Actually childless –

forever. Then you'll never be a mother."

"God, stop."

"You need to think about it," Cecilie says. "And the risk of HIV." Her voice is suddenly harsh. "You don't know who else he's been with."

Something turns unpleasantly in my gut. *I've only ever done it before when I was drunk*, he said, and now I'm wondering if that means he's been with a different girl at every party, if you even remember to use protection if you're drunk and horny. And anyway why would I fall in love with someone who acts in such a totally gross, unhygienic fashion?

I try to make my irritation go away, turning my head and brushing my hair until it crackles with static. When I shake my hair back into place and look at myself in the mirror, Cecilie is still standing there.

"You look beautiful," she says.

I stare at my reflection. "Thanks."

She's biting a nail, leaning against the door frame. Then, abruptly, there are tears in her eyes. I go over and put my arms round her. She starts to cry in earnest. My top is getting damp with snot and tears. I'll have to change it in a minute, and that shouldn't be what I'm focused on, but it is.

"I just didn't think things would be like this," she sobs. "So difficult. So insanely difficult."

I don't know what to say so I just hold her.

"I can't do anything right."

"Yes, you can. Stop that, OK?"

I check my watch behind her neck as I'm hugging her. There's only an hour before Kristoffer comes out of the exam room.

"Do you think I'm a bad person?"

"Why would I think that?"

She pulls away and makes an attempt to dry her face with her bare forearms. "It's so weird you're going to see *him* graduate," she says. "I feel … I really feel…"

"You feel like it should have been you I'm going to see," I finish for her. It just slips out of me – I don't have the time for her to speak and feel this slowly.

"Yeah." Her eyes blink swiftly, surprised.

"And I will do one day," I say, picking up my bag from the desk, checking for my keys, my phone.

"Do you want to come and sit with me in the garden for a bit?" she asks.

"Now?!"

"Yeah?" She stares at me emptily, as though she's already deleted from her brain what we talked about literally thirty seconds ago.

"I'm going to see Kristoffer get his graduation cap. Yeah?"

"I forgot."

I look at my sister – no, I stare. It's like everything that's been building over the last couple of years rises up inside me like a big evil wave. *No, you didn't*, I think. *You're just trying to manipulate me into staying here with you because you don't want me to go out and live my life. You won't be satisfied until every member of this family is as stuck as you are, will you?*

I try to squeeze out a smile but it feels too small, too fake. She turns her face away. Flops down on to my bed with a sigh.

"When are you coming home?"

"I don't know."

"Two hours?"

"Depends how long it takes to eat strawberries and marzipan cake and do the champagne toasts and stuff like that."

I'm not trying to be mean – I just have to buttress my explanation.

Cecilie stares at me, saying nothing.

I pull off my snot- and tear-stained jumper, throw it on the floor and hurriedly rummage through my wardrobe, finding a clean top, putting it on and tucking it into my trousers.

"See you."

I give her a hug while she's sitting down and she holds on tight; it feels like she's never going to let go. Finally she removes her arms and I'm almost out of the room when she says, "You always used to ask me if I wanted to come with you when you were going out. You don't any more."

I stop short. Swallow once. "Do you want to come?"

"No. But you shouldn't ever stop asking."

She stretches her arms towards me, wanting another cuddle. But suddenly I can't handle the thought of being close to her again. I need to get out of here right now.

"Gotta run. See you later."

Kristoffer's mum is outside the examination room on the first floor. There are a couple of guys from his class too, including the one with the piercing, Fillip. Luckily he's busy talking to some of the others. Ellen says it's lovely I've come but we don't hug. She seems nervous, and maybe it's because of the dumb conversation we had the other day, or maybe it's just because of the atmosphere in the hallway. It's only a minute or two before I catch them too, the red cheeks and legs that won't stay still.

"Are you coming back with us to celebrate tonight?" she asks.

"I've still got to figure that out," I say, thinking of Cecilie asking me to hurry back.

Kristoffer emerges from the exam room five minutes later. He runs both hands through his black hair and pulls a face, then comes straight up to me and gives me such a fierce hug that I'm lifted off the ground and we nearly do a twirl.

"I got the fucking Vietnam War," he says with his arms still round me. He sounds happy and he smells faintly of sweat and I want to bury my head in his armpit.

"You did the best you could and now it's over. You'll be graduating soon – think about that." Ellen rubs his back.

An invigilator walks past and shushes us. Then the door opens, and the history teacher calls Kristoffer in. A few minutes pass. Ellen shuffles in little circles. Then he reappears, throws out his arms and says, "Ten!"

Everybody laughs and shouts congratulations, including me, and I get out my phone and take a picture the moment the red-and-white cap touches his head.

As I'm putting my phone away, I realize Mum sent me a text.

Thought you were going to be home today?

That must mean my sister called or texted to say she's alone. I type quickly.

Went to see Kristoffer get his graduation cap.

Mum doesn't reply. It feels like a reproach she knows she can't justifiably say out loud so she just squeezes it out through her silence.

Right there, suddenly, I've had enough. I'm seized by how unreasonable it is that I'm not allowed to stand here and be happy on Kristoffer's behalf without feeling like I'm letting my mother and my sister down.

Going back with him to celebrate tonight, I write.

Probably be home late.

OK. Have fun.

The guilt is back, like a punch to the gut. It's nobody's fault my sister is ill. We're all trapped in it and Mum just wants Cecilie to feel safe. I'm about to text back and ask if Cecilie is OK, if I should come home. But then Kristoffer smiles at me and I let my phone slip back into my bag, deciding to stay right where I am.

There are loads of kids from my sister's class getting their caps today, but we still manage to find a free space upstairs in the Sink. Ellen sets out plastic glasses on the tables and invites everybody who stops and says congratulations to stay and drink a toast with us. We end up with a collection of nearly twenty people drinking champagne and eating strawberries dipped in chocolate. Somebody opens the door to the roof terrace and soon people are drifting outdoors into the sunshine.

I go outside too. At first I stick close to Kristoffer, but of course everybody wants to talk to him, so I start mingling by myself a bit. Eventually I bump into Fillip.

"Whaddaya say – we gonna be friends?" He bumps his plastic glass against mine, taking a drag from the cigarette in his other hand.

"Sure, yeah." The champagne must be taking effect because I muster a smile.

"Nice," he says, laughing. "So no hard feelings?"

"No hard feelings," I say, although I'm not sure that's the truth. "When are you done?"

"I did mine on Monday. I just don't fancy running around like an idiot with that cap." He takes another drag of his cigarette and stares over my head, as though he's looking for someone. "Now we just have to power through tomorrow."

"What's happening tomorrow?" I ask.

"Didn't you know?" He blows a perfect smoke ring into the air. "Party at Kristoffer's. Maybe, if you're lucky, he'll let you drop by." He adds with a sly grin, "If you ask him really nicely..."

I know exactly how stupid and childish I must come across. How unserious the thing between me and Kristoffer must seem, given that he doesn't even tell me stuff like that.

"I've got another party to go to tomorrow," I say.

"Shame." Fillip smiles, putting the cigarette back between his lips.

Kristoffer's granddad shows up for dinner that evening too and the four of us sit out in the garden, clinking glasses with the sun on our faces. At some point, Kristoffer's dad phones and he goes indoors to take the call, returning two minutes later.

"He says hi." He sits back down and pours more wine for himself and me.

"Thanks." Ellen sets down her cutlery, carefully placing the fork slantwise across the knife and taking a short pause before she says, "Is he sticking to the plan? Will he be coming on Friday?"

"No." Kristoffer puts his fork in his mouth, chews, looks down at his plate. "Something came up."

Ellen and Sven exchange a brief glance.

"I'll probably go up and visit him for a couple of days in August. When it's convenient."

By the time we go upstairs, I've drunk two glasses of wine and I'm feeling warm and giddy. I'd wanted to ask Kristoffer about his dad but then we just tumble on to his bed and kiss until I'm even more dizzy and need to ask for a glass of water. As soon as he's gone downstairs to find something to drink in the kitchen, I sit up. Take out my phone. The blank screen makes my pulse thud slow and hard. I consider sending Cecilie a heart but it doesn't feel like a crappy little heart is going to be much help.

When Kristoffer returns with a jug of water and two glasses, he smiles brightly.

"What?" I say.

"I was just thinking that I've graduated now, I'm on holiday, I'm free, and I've got *you* sitting here." He knocks me backwards and lies on top of me.

"It'll be easier now too," he says.

"What will be easier?"

"Us seeing each other. It's been a bit random so far, don't you think?"

Of all the words, he has to use 'random'.

I push him off and sit up. "Why didn't you tell me you're having a party tomorrow?"

He shrugs. Getting up, he pours a glass of water and hands it to me. "I didn't think about it. I mean, it's just a party."

"For who?"

"My class."

I take a big gulp of water. The idea that there are going to be drunk, noisy people all over his house tomorrow night makes me feel weird.

"I guess you'll be busy then," I say. "Buying drinks and decorating and cleaning up after."

"Decorating?" He laughs – it feels like a mocking laugh. "There are only three rules: you bring your own booze, no making a mess, and if you're going to fuck or throw up you go into the garden. That's it."

"Charming."

"Just be glad you don't have to watch." He sits down and leans forward to kiss me, but I dodge him.

"And it's just for your class?"

"Yeah." He looks a bit surprised at my question. "Did you want to come?"

"Nope."

"What's wrong? Are you jealous?" He smiles. Like an arsehole.

"I mean, it's not great that you told me you're used to smashing a bunch of girls when you're drunk."

"Actually, I never feel much like smashing when I'm drunk," he says, forcing his fingers between mine. "Usually some girl manages to talk me round."

"OK, that makes it much better." I tear my hand free. "You do realize you're risking making me childless?"

"What?!" He laughs loudly.

I pull a sulky face.

"Come here, silly."

He pulls me close and draws the duvet over our heads.

It doesn't take long in the dark before I've forgotten he was an arsehole. Soon he's peeled off my sweater, then my bra. He goes to open my trousers but I grab his wrist and stop him.

"I have condoms," he says.

"It feels weird when there are other people in the house."

"They'll survive. The door's shut. Or are you a screamer?"

I elbow him and he laughs. Then he pulls my underwear aside, bites my earlobe and runs his finger back and forth. All the while I'm breathing very quietly. There's a rushing in my ears.

I have to say it now. "I haven't slept with anyone before."

His fingers stop moving. He stares at me. Somehow he seems taken aback, disappointed. I can't work out what.

"But I want to," I say quickly. "With you."

Afterwards, we lie there, looking out of the slanting window. The sky never gets really black on summer nights; even the darkness feels bright.

"Are you OK with your dad not coming to your graduation ceremony?" I ask.

"Mm," he says.

"You won't be sad?"

"Mostly it's my mum who'll be disappointed. On my behalf. I'd rather have him cancel than show up and not be able to cope."

"It's great you can think that way," I say.

"What else should I be thinking? Nobody benefits from people overstepping their own limitations."

He's smiling but I'm finding it hard to swallow. Why can't I look at my sister in the same reasonable way? What's wrong with me? I sit up and try to figure out in the dim light where my clothes landed.

"Aren't you going to sleep over?" He pulls me close to him again so I'm lying with my head on his upper arm.

"I promised Cecilie I'd come home."

My mum's texts pop into my head. My sister's expression when she asked me to hurry back. It's dark now. She'll be in bed. How has her day been?

Kristoffer lifts his head and looks at me. "You know you're not helping her by being like this, right?"

"Like what?"

"Like a security blanket."

"OK, fuck you. You don't know what helps her."

He lets his head fall back and strokes my hair, as though to apologize. "The thing she's got can't be fixed by you being there. You're not the cure, are you?"

"There isn't any hundred-per-cent cure."

"No. But we agree that *you're* not it?"

I can tell I'm not in any state to discuss this with him again. "Mm," is all I say.

He rolls on to his back and yawns. "But go home to her

if it'll make you feel better."

I shuffle to the edge of the bed and fish out my phone, writing a quick text to my mum to say I'm going to stay the night and that I hope they've had an all right day.

"Right then. You're going to get your way," I say.

I wake early the next morning, listening to all the strange noises: Kristoffer's mum humming loudly along to the radio downstairs; the sputtering coffee machine in the kitchen; doors being opened and closed. Moments later, she bustles up the stairs, knocks on the door and says, "I'm setting off now – you two have fun!"

Kristoffer wakes up. We cuddle together. I can smell sweat and cologne on the soft, dark hair of his armpits. His hips feel angular against my body. His dick is hard, his chin scratchy. Everything about him is so different from me, it's overwhelming.

"We agree you're here of your own free will, right?" he says hoarsely.

"Yeah."

"I didn't kidnap you or force you to do anything, did I?"

"No." I can't help laughing a bit.

"But you're crying?" He runs his finger along the arc of my cheek, mopping up the wetness.

"I don't know why."

"Because you're very, very happy?" he suggests.

My eyes fall on the digital clock on his bedside table. It's nearly nine. I slip out of his grip and find my phone on the floor. Mum's called three times. No doubt she'll be wanting me to come home and hang out with Cecilie so she can go to work with a clear conscience. I'm about to ring back when Kristoffer snatches the phone out of my hand and shoves it under his pillow.

"There!" he says. "Now let's make breakfast."

We don't say goodbye until twelve, after we've sat in his little square garden and drunk coffee and eaten pancakes, until his neighbour, who's evidently a childminder, lets out all five kids, and they start destroying a sandpit while screaming and shouting.

"Hope you have a good party tonight," I say, standing on the doorstep.

He leans against the frame. The look he gives me makes me want to stay there forever. I never want to be looked at in any other way by any other person.

"You're sure you don't want to come?" He reaches out and

runs his fingers down my arm.

"It's OK… It's your party." I smile at him. "We'll text?" I ask before I can stop myself.

"Unless one of us dies."

"Why would you say a thing like that?"

"Sorry." He smiles. "I'm just a bit weird. Are you coming to graduation?"

"I have to help decorate the trucks," I say. "Like everybody else in my year."

"Well then, we'll see each other there." He tosses his head nonchalantly, as though our goodbye is a bit ridiculous, a bit unnecessary. "And obviously we'll see each other afterwards."

"Afterwards," I repeat in the same nonchalant way. "Sure."

I can't help feeling a little bubble of anticipation in my stomach as I walk away.

Afterwards.

All the things that could be waiting after that word.

When I reach my house, the bubble bursts and my stomach tightens back up. The door is locked; no windows are open. I have to let myself in. Silence is oozing out of every room in the house. I go round and check everywhere: empty.

Then I call Cecilie. There's a buzzing from her room – the phone is vibrating on the floor under the bed.

My heart starts thudding a bit harder. Mum isn't picking up the phone either. So I try my dad. He answers just as I'm about to give up.

"Hello?" As he picks up, I remember the last time I called, when he was sitting in a meeting and was annoyed at both of us because he hadn't put his phone on silent.

"Dad? Sorry – I'm calling." The words pitch out in odd jerks. "Do you know – where Cecilie is?"

"Mum's been trying to get hold of you for ages."

"I know but I—"

"We're at the emergency department," he interrupts. "We'll come home once we've spoken to a doctor. Hopefully it won't be long."

"What happened?"

He's breathing heavily. His voice is low. "It's the *psychiatric* emergency department."

I feel dizzy. I don't know what to say. I can hear my mum in the background now, telling my dad something that makes him shush her before he speaks to me again.

"Don't panic."

"But has something happened? To Cecilie?"

"You mustn't worry," he says after a moment's silence. "We'll talk about it when we get home, Astrid. OK?"

Guilt rushes through my veins like a powerful drug, making me light-headed and sick.

I run to the kitchen and retch into the sink. Then I hurry into Cecilie's room, throw the duvet aside, check under the bed, in her bag, rummage through the drawers for pill bottles. Nothing but a single, almost-full blister pack of paracetamol in the middle of the mess on her desk.

Still I don't feel reassured.

Everything she's said and done, all the warning signs I didn't want to look at, they're all flashing at me now: *"I've got such a weird feeling that everything will be over soon anyway."*

I grab her laptop, shut all the windows showing movies and click on her search history. And suddenly they're in front of me, in a long list: words, sentences. Just not about suicide.

Hidden heart defect symptoms

Congenital heart defect

Lung cancer symptoms

Sclerosis symptoms

Foetal malformation

HIV from blood transfusion

HIV from the doctor's

HIV from a public toilet

Stepping on HIV syringe

What does choking feel like?

What does drowning feel like?

Surviving a plane crash

Worst death toll plane crash

Terror attack 9/11

Chlamydia symptoms

Chlamydia childlessness

HIV symptoms

HIV from oral sex

HIV cut in mouth

Motor neuron disease symptoms

Septicaemia symptoms

Pain at top of lung

Blood clot in the lung

The words just keep going and going. The history goes back months, and I can see her searching for the same things again and again: illness, death, accidents, illness, death, accidents. I realize that this is what she spends her time staring at whenever I'm not with her. This is the stuff she feeds her brain every single night.

Everything we do for her, and then she lies there, staring at this shit, going against our advice, wallowing in death, illness and pain so she can feel even more anxiety, even more panic.

I smack the computer shut and push it back under the bed.

I wait for them to come home.

The car rolls up the driveway around four. They get out. Cecilie walks at a slow, somnambulatory pace. Mum's arm is round her waist, supporting her, as though she's got a broken leg or a sprained foot.

If we were an ordinary family, this would be the moment we'd sit down together and have a cup of afternoon coffee while they asked how Kristoffer's last exam went. And I'd tell them how happy he was, how we ate langoustines with a mountain of garlic butter last night, how we made pancakes this morning.

But, as usual, I keep all my experiences to myself. I go back to my room as they let themselves in. I can hear them walking down the hall, into Cecilie's room, and shutting the door. Murmuring, muted voices. Something that sounds like apathetic crying. Only twenty minutes later do my parents re-emerge. I'm still listening at the door.

Dad says he has to go into the office and get a few hours' work done.

Mum says nothing.

Seconds later, the front door slams. The car starts in the driveway. I leave my room. Find Mum outside on the terrace. She's sitting with her feet up on one of the garden chairs, staring at the flowerpots with a rigid gaze.

"Mum?"

She jumps at the sound of my voice.

"What happened to Cecilie?"

She takes a deep breath. "Oh well … it was just a really, really bad night. And this morning she was completely out of it. She… Dad had to carry her to the car when—"

"*Carry* her?"

I picture it: Dad holding my sister like a baby as he walks down the garden path, placing her on the back seat, clicking the seat belt gently across her body. Mum stroking Cecilie's cheek, whispering to her reassuringly. And I know I should feel concern and sympathy but I actually feel like I'm about to explode.

"It'll be better now," Mum says, looking like she's hoping someone will leap out from behind the hedge and back her up. "We spoke to a great doctor. Cecilie is going to get referred to a psychiatrist so she can be properly examined and then she'll start on medication straight away to minimize the symptoms of anxiety."

I'm sure my dad is even angrier and more disappointed than he was already. I'm sure we'll be walking on eggshells round my sister even more now. And what if she gets some of the side effects Dad's always droning on about? Puts on twenty kilos and gets depressed about it? Or what if she won't go to the psychiatrist? Will they keep carrying her around like a little kid?

Mum gives me a dull smile. "Cecilie did so well when we got there. She told the doctor all about her thoughts. She was very honest."

I say, "Well, isn't that great?"

Mum doesn't notice anything. She just keeps talking. "Cecilie also said she was considering dropping the make-up exams and redoing the third year. We didn't finish talking about that, of course. But maybe it really would be best. She's missed a lot of classes, after all. Perhaps this will be a fresh start for her."

Another year of texts from the toilet.

Another year of setting off early in the morning because my sister's legs don't move at the same speed as everyone else's.

Another year of encouraging, supporting, helping.

"I actually think it's a sign of maturity that she can see that for herself. Dad disagrees, of course." She waves her hand as though there's a fly buzzing too close. "But that's not something we should discuss at this point either. Right now, we just have to concentrate on being there for her."

My sisters sleeps the day away. Dad comes home, we manage to sit down in the kitchen and eat potato salad with sausages fried in a pan, and she still hasn't woken up.

Dad is shovelling down his food. Mum's knife and fork are on her plate. She doesn't eat but she doesn't say anything either; there are no remarks about the weather or the temperature of the sea. I find it hard to swallow the food. The cracked lumps of sausage on my plate bob around in ketchup and mayonnaise from the potato salad.

After five minutes, Dad gets up. "Right! I think I'm going out for a run. You coming, Astrid?"

It doesn't sound like a friendly offer. It sounds like there's going to be a fight and now's the time to pick a team.

"No thanks."

"Really? All right, then I'll run by myself!" He drops his plate into the sink with a crash, leaves the kitchen, comes back in running clothes two minutes later and disappears out through the door.

Mum rests her head in her hands and stares down at her plate for a few seconds, before looking up, giving me a twisted smile and emptying her glass of water. "Sausages aren't really all that nice if they're not grilled, are they?" she says.

I think about texting Jonas.

My family's gone full-blown mental at last.

But sadly we don't send each other texts like that any more.

I can't bring myself to go into her room until half past eight. Part of me hopes she's still asleep. That the toilet door I heard creak twenty minutes ago just means she got up to pee, then went back to bed.

But now she's wide awake. She's up, in fact, in front of the mirror, brushing her hair with long strokes and a pink brush.

It's such a shock to see her standing there that for a moment I get this feeling like she's not my sister.

"Hi," I say.

She doesn't answer. Just keeps brushing.

"I'm sorry to hear you … about what happened yesterday. This morning. Mum told me."

She still says nothing. The brushstrokes crackle.

I take a deep breath. "I hope they were—"

"I don't want to talk about it."

I sit down on the bed, picking at a small hole in the sheet, widening it with my finger. "Mum says you're thinking of redoing the third year?"

"I haven't decided yet."

"But can you cope with another whole year of school?"

"I don't know." She brushes her hair more vigorously. *Krat-krat-krat*, every time the bristles scrape across her scalp.

"Then what do you want to do?"

"I'll figure it out. There are several options."

It's totally absurd to hear my sister using a word like 'options'.

"But do you think you've actually got it in you to redo a whole year?" I ask. "Do you think it will make things better?"

"Yes."

"OK." I just sit and watch her for a minute. Then I say, "I'm only asking because I don't think so."

Her lips contract. In fact, her whole face contracts as I stare at it in the mirror.

"Yeah, well, thanks for your opinion," she says.

"I'm just trying to help you."

She brushes even harder, even quicker. Fine fair hairs swirl through the air and drift towards the floor.

I say, "If there's something wrong, you can say so. Instead of just standing there, looking pissed off."

She keeps brushing, keeps looking pissed off.

I get off the bed. "To be honest, I just came in here to be nice."

She scowls at me in the mirror. "Well, that's great, thanks. I'm *trying*, I'm *fighting*, but it's obvious you need to tell me I can't."

My heart starts hammering at double speed. My whole body is tense and hot and ready.

"Are you serious?" I say. "You can't even walk on your own two feet, but I'm supposed to believe you can redo a whole year?"

"Fuck, you're horrible." There are tears in her eyes. "Do you think this is something I chose? To be like this?"

"I don't know," I say, thinking about all the things she spends her nights googling. "But you could at least try to do something yourself. *Try* to turn up to your therapy sessions; *try* to take an exam. Try to think a positive thought. What's the worst thing that can happen? That you fail? So what! Loads of people fail, but they move on. *Everybody* has shit to go through."

She's standing utterly still, rigid. At first I think she's decided to give me the silent treatment. But then she turns towards me, burning red in the face. "It must be lovely to be as perfect as you. Always doing the right thing. Always making Mum and Dad happy."

Rage kicks its way out of my belly and I feel like now it's come, it's never going to let me go. "You think *I* have a perfect life? Do you really think I like being your crutch most of the time?!"

"Get out!" she yells. "Get out of my room!"

I head for the door but before I leave I'm struck by something in the back of my neck. A hard, astonishing stab of pain. When I turn back, I catch sight of the pink hairbrush on the floor. Then I look up and meet Cecilie's eyes. Tears are running down her cheeks. Her whole face is twisted.

"I hate my life!" she says. "I hate myself!"

I put my hand to my neck. As small as she looks now, I still feel angry.

"I can't help you," I say.

Her bottom lip is quivering. For a moment, I feel sorry for her. Then I harden myself again.

"Stay here," she says. "Please. Just be here with me." She stretches out her arms towards me.

Everything inside me shrinks at the sight of those arms.

"It's because you can't deal with me getting a life," I say. "Isn't it? You're angry because I don't want to keep lying here, gawping at a screen with you every single day."

"No." She shakes her head several times. The tears are still pouring down her cheeks. "It's because you're the only person in the entire world who really understands me. You're the only one who makes me believe I'm all right. And I feel like I'm losing you."

"But I want to try and be happy too! I want to be with Kristoffer. I want to travel with my friends. I can't *just* be here. Don't you get that?!"

We're both gasping for breath.

"You can't go out with him," she says.

"Stop it."

"You'll be sorry."

There's something desperate in her voice that makes my heart pound twice as fast.

"No, I won't!"

"You will," she says. "He'll make you sad somehow. He'll cheat on you. Or leave. What is he doing for his gap year?"

"Shut up!" I say. "Just shut the fuck up!"

I can't stand anything about this house any longer. Not my mum or my dad or my sister. It's like they're all spiralling down a massive hole and now they're pulling me into it as well.

I run out of the room. Mum is standing in the hallway – she must have been listening by the door. She tries to catch my arm, saying, "What's going on, Astrid?"

But I knock her hand aside and race into the kitchen, into the garden, away.

As I walk down the street, my whole body is shaking. I take out my phone and call Kristoffer. I need to hear his voice.

He doesn't pick up.

I break off the call just before it goes through to the answering machine, then try ringing again. He still isn't answering. My heart is thudding, my mouth is dry and I can't feel like this for two seconds longer. I text him:

Please call!

And another one:

I need to talk to you!

Mum keeps trying to get hold of me but I hurriedly decline the call every time, in case Kristoffer is trying to get through. I imagine he'll ask me to come over as soon as he sees my texts. That he'll meet me in the road outside his house, leave the party, hold me and talk to me for the rest of the night.

But of course he has to call first.

I head in the direction of his place. Two streets away I sit down on the pavement and wait. You can hear the party from here. A constant thudding bass. My phone remains silent.

I text Jonas:

Really need someone to talk to right now.

He doesn't answer. Perhaps he's already asleep.

I wait nearly twenty minutes but Kristoffer still hasn't replied. Then I wait another ten and now it's been nearly an hour since I first called.

When I get to my feet, I know I've no intention of going home.

There are two girls I don't recognize standing smoking outside Kristoffer's house, all dolled up. They ignore me as

I walk past. Inside the music is so loud it makes my ears ring. I push through the crowds of people in the living room and the garden but he's nowhere to be found and it's clear this is not just a class party – there are way more than thirty people here, more like twice that. On the way back out through the kitchen, I bump into Fillip.

"*He-e-ey!*" he yells, giving me a half hug, half shoulder bump. "You did come!"

"Do you know where Kristoffer is?"

His mouth is really close to my ear but he's still yelling. "He's in the middle of a really serious conversation with Liv upstairs!"

"Liv?" I shout back. "Who's Liv?"

"Girl who's just been dumped way too hard by her boyfriend!" He laughs as though there's something funny about it. "What shall we get for you? Whisky and Coke? Shots?"

I don't answer. I've already turned to leave when Fillip grabs my arm. "Hey! You can't disturb them right now."

Tearing myself free with a jerk, I force my way towards the stairs. There's a couple kissing on the middle steps and I have to edge past. The door to Kristoffer's room is shut. I consider knocking but only for a second, then I just fling it open.

He's sitting on the bed. Next to him is a girl who must be Liv. They're sitting so close their thighs touch, and it doesn't seem to bother either of them. Not one bit.

"Hey? Astrid?"

It's the astonishment in his face that hits me. The fear of losing him feels like someone is squashing the air out of my lungs.

"What are you doing here?" He stands up.

"I called you." My voice is cracking. "And texted."

He walks towards me. I'm hit by a strange wave of booze and cigarette smoke I've never smelled on him before.

"I didn't see," he says. "What happened?"

"Can we talk? Alone?"

"Yeah… OK…" He turns towards the not-sad girl on the bed, saying, "Back in a minute."

I don't want to be humiliated further by hearing her response. I just turn my back and start walking, barging down the stairs, nearly kicking the stomach-turning couple who are still making out, nearly giving the finger to the two girls outside, who shoot us sly stares as we pass.

"What are you doing here?" he repeats once we're standing on the pavement outside. The street lamps don't illuminate this bit but the moon still shows me his face.

"I really needed to see you," I say.

He doesn't give me a hug. He just stands there in front of me with his arms hanging by his sides, as though he's forgotten what he usually uses them for when we see each other.

I take a deep breath. "My parents drove Cecilie to the psychiatric ward this morning, and we've just had a massive fight, me and her I mean, and I said, I said some things like – you know, things you can't—"

"Psychiatric ward, what? Slower."

I stare at him. He's swaying slightly.

"Sorry," he says. "It's just you're talking way too fast. You're saying a lot of words, OK?" And then he smiles crookedly, as though the whole thing's a joke for him.

Suddenly I can see that Cecilie has been right this whole time. He might act nice and say he wants to make me happy, but he's really just a superficial idiot.

"Why are there so many people here?" I ask. "Wasn't it supposed to be a *class* party?"

He shrugs. "People bring friends. It happens."

"And why were you all alone up in your room? You and that…" I really have to pull myself together not to call her something seriously ugly. "*Girl?*"

"Did you come here to check up on me?" Suddenly he sounds angry. Then he changes his mind. "That's Liv."

"Doesn't she have any female friends to comfort her, if she's so sad?"

"I'm her friend," he says. "Weren't you the one who told me girls and boys could be friends?"

"So you've never slept with her? You're *just* friends?"

"Yeah," he says. "Or no. What should I say so you don't get cross?"

"You should be honest."

"Then yes. I mean no. What was the question again?"

He puts his hand on a lamp post, leaning against it; he's

about to lose his balance, but then finds it again.

"How drunk *are* you?" I ask.

"Out of my skull," he replies.

"Is it fun getting hammered and just stumbling around without a brain?"

"Um, yeah." He smiles that idiotic smile again. "I'm with my friends, I've downed a bottle of tequila, and yeah, it's actually pretty fun. You should try it."

He takes a step forward, trying at last to get his arms round my waist, but it's too late now. I push him off.

"You *stink*. Why didn't you say you were a social smoker?"

"Why didn't you say you were so boring?"

"I can't be bothered with this," I say. "Just go back to your party."

"Wow, thank you so much."

I can't ignore his sarcastic tone of voice. "Just go upstairs and have sex with someone else if that's what you want. I don't care."

He grabs my shoulder before I turn on my heel. "What the hell is wrong with you tonight?"

"I'm not interested in being a laughing stock."

"What? I'm not allowed to talk to other girls?"

"I just don't like the thought of you getting drunk and sleeping with someone else."

"Hang on a minute," he says. "You're the one I'm crazy about. I've told you that a million times, Astrid. Jesus." His voice softens. Becomes more like himself. "But you can't just march in here and… I'm at a party now, OK?" He lets go of my arm. "Can we talk about this tomorrow?"

"I don't know."

Part of me wants to cry and cling to him and beg him to promise that what we've got is eternal and that nothing and no one can ever tear us apart. But I know that's not a thing any human can promise – especially after such a short time. So I try to harden everything about myself, inside and out. He searches my face with his eyes. I can feel them crawling round, scanning for a crack or a crevice. At last he realizes there isn't one.

"So what now?" He throws out his arms.

I say: "I think maybe we're just very different people."

He snorts. "You know exactly what kind of person I am."

"That's not what I mean," I say. "You're just … I thought you could make me happy but you can't."

For a moment, I'm sure that's that.

That he'll turn round and go back into the house.

Then he says, "Jesus, this is ridiculous! *This* is how much you give of yourself." He shows how little with the space between his thumb and index finger. "I get *this* much to work with all the time but I'm supposed to just give and give and tell you how much I want you, is that how it is?!"

His chest is rising and falling rapidly. His eyes are wide.

I take a step back, away from him.

"It was just a mistake from the beginning, this," I say. "A giant mistake."

That's the last thing I say to him. Then I turn and go. I continue past all the small, identical terraced houses. Past the driveways of sleeping cars. I pass a dog-walker but otherwise it's deserted. Kristoffer doesn't come running after me. Nobody calls.

I just walk down the road, sobbing.

I call Jonas three times in a row, but he doesn't pick up. Then I call Veronica.

"Hello?" She sounds drowsy, like she was sleeping.

"Is Jonas with you?"

"What?"

"It's Astrid!" I shout. "Is Jonas there?"

"Jonas isn't here… Are you crying?"

"No!"

"You can come to my place," she says very gently. "If you're upset."

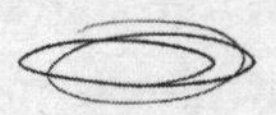

What's crazy is that I accept her offer. What's weird is that my legs take me down roads I've never walked before.

Veronica lets me in through the utility-room door, saying her parents and little brothers are asleep, and we walk upstairs in silence. We shut the door. I'm on a beanbag chair that makes my body fold up, Veronica on her bed in floral pyjamas. The walls are green. The place smells of lavender, a holiday-cottage scent.

I try to explain my evening to her, avoiding the lead-up and skipping straight to the party and my conversation with Kristoffer.

"And now he's definitely with somebody else," I say. "Because people don't like being accused of things they haven't done. So they just do them."

"Of course he's not with someone else." She has a way of saying these things that makes you believe her. "Why don't you trust him?"

"I just don't think he's the person I thought he was."

"Don't you think we all go around with a slightly wrong impression of each other?" She goes a little pink in the cheeks and glances away from me. "But if you like him, I mean, it would be stupid not to think the best of him."

Her words make me curl up my arms and legs in the beanbag chair, trying to disappear inside it.

"Everything is just shit right now," I say.

She's quiet a moment. "Jonas mentioned you're under a lot of pressure at home..."

"What did he say?"

"Just that your sister isn't well. Anxiety, is it?"

It's totally obvious that she knows full well it's anxiety and that Jonas didn't just mention it once in passing. Clearly, he's been complaining about me and my relationship with Cecilie the entire time Veronica's known him. If I know my best friend, probably not a day has passed without him whining about it.

"Mental illness isn't like a broken leg," I say. "You can't fix it."

"What's being done to help her?"

"Everything. Seriously we're doing *everything*!"

"Everything?" She adjusts her glasses. "That sounds like kind of a lot."

"But she doesn't *want* to be healthy," I say. "She spends all her time googling all the shit that makes her anxious. HIV and cancer and stuff like that. Isn't that crazy?!"

"Sure," says Veronica. "It's pretty crazy. But isn't that why it's an illness?"

When she says it, it almost makes sense.

"This has just been the worst, shittiest month of my life!" I remember Kristoffer and correct myself. "Almost. And I have this pain in my stomach the whole time. And my parents don't know how I'm doing, or they don't care. And Jonas doesn't either."

"Maybe you should try saying this to your family," Veronica says, totally ignoring what I said about Jonas. "So they know how you're doing."

"It's just not really my style to moan about stuff," I say.

"It's not moaning to tell people how you feel. And if I were your parents, I'd want to know."

"You don't know my family. My dad is totally—"

She interrupts me. "Sometimes you need to give people a chance to show you their best side."

That makes me fall silent for a while.

"At first I didn't like you," I say at last. "I think maybe I was a bit jealous of you."

"There's not much to be jealous of," she says. "I'm pretty ordinary."

"I made Jonas call you 'Veronicaraptor' when you started school. Just to be mean."

She looks at me for a few long seconds without blinking. It's hard to tell what she's thinking. Probably that I'm a complete twat.

"Are you and Jonas dating?" I ask.

"Nah. We're taking it slow." It sounds quite a lot like a chilled-out Veronica version of, "Yes, till death do us part."

"You can't forget about me."

She says, "I think actually Jonas is the one who feels like you've forgotten him."

"Seriously?! He takes like a thousand years to text back. He acts as if he couldn't care less about me."

"Hm," she says, biting her bottom lip.

"What?"

I can tell that Jonas has said something about me that she isn't keen to pass on.

"Sometimes I think he feels like you only want to hang out when it suits you. When you have a problem." She looks at me through half-closed eyes. "I think he wishes you'd show that you're there for him too."

"Of course I'm there for him."

"OK, but ... like, you were too busy studying to bother showing up to his exam. And you forgot the anniversary of his dad's death. A week ago."

"Fuck."

The very first day I met Jonas he told me his dad had died during a friendly with the neighbouring town five years ago. One moment he was running around, kicking the ball, shouting and screaming at his opponents, and the next he collapsed with a heart attack. Dead on the spot. Jonas also said his mum and brothers went to the churchyard every year on the twentieth of June and heaped the grave with flowers and the bucket hats his dad always wore in the summer. I marked the date in my calendar ages ago and I would have liked to give him a hug and a hat to take with him. Instead I completely forgot.

"I think maybe you should say something about it soon," Veronica continues. "So it doesn't turn into some big thing between you."

"Thanks. I will."

Veronica looks round the room as though assessing the narrow space between the bed, the beanbag chair and the little desk.

"Shall I fetch our extra mattress?"

When we're lying in the dark and I think she's fallen asleep, she says abruptly, "But getting back to Kristoffer, I think you should call him tomorrow and just say you're sorry about the way you acted. Ask him if you can be friends again. Or whatever you guys are."

"Cute," I say. "But that stuff about second chances only works in romcoms. Reality isn't like that. Not when you've only known each other as short a time as we have."

"You do have some impact on how reality works out, you know," she says.

The next morning I wake at half five, as the first rays of dawn are filtering through the window. As soon as I realize where I am, I feel like bursting into tears again.

Mum's called several times and sent me texts over the course of the night.

Please could you ring back?

I'm assuming you're sleeping over at Kristoffer's?

Please give me some sign of life??

And then she sent a text at five in the morning, asking if I could possibly be home by half eight at the latest because that's when she needs to leave, and Cecilie has been up most of the night and would be better off not on her own.

If you can, she writes, followed by a heart.

I force snot and tears back down my throat with a rather unattractive noise.

"Are you awake?" Veronica pokes her head over the edge of the bed. Her eyes look small and mole-like without glasses. "Shall we sleep a bit more?"

"I think I should go home."

"Now?" she says. "Don't you want breakfast first? We could bake rolls?"

"I'd rather not meet your family right now. Um, I mean, if that's OK."

I leave the house with a cheese sandwich I have no intention of eating but I don't have the heart to say I can't stand cheese, and definitely not cheese with such a strong fungus-y smell like the one Veronica carefully slices before pressing the sandwich into my hand.

"There you go," she says. "And I'll see you when we decorate the trucks tomorrow, right?"

"Yeah. And thanks." I hesitate in the doorway a moment, dispirited at the thought of the mess that's waiting for me once I leave.

"Good luck with everything." She nudges me gently outside and shuts the door behind me.

Once upon a time, when we were little, my sister was my whole world. It was how I felt watching her as we ate breakfast and she sat rubbing sleep out of her eyes and I recognized her movements as my own. And there were days of which I remember nothing but my big sister. There was only Astrid and Cecilie. We needed no one else, and every time I turned round she was there.

I don't know why things can't stay as simple as when we were kids. Why you have to wake up and realize that your sister, who once could do everything, no longer can. That your family might not be as strong as you thought it was. That there are things that can't be fixed.

When I think about what's happened to our family, I don't know if it can ever fully be repaired. And, yeah, it's not like anyone is dying. But I don't want to be the person who tries to hold all this stuff together any more. I don't want to pretend that I can really make the difference by myself.

The house is asleep when I let myself in. I put the kettle on, settling to stare out of the window. As the water reaches a boil, I hear the familiar creak of my parents' bedroom door. Seconds later, Mum is standing in the doorway in her dressing gown.

"I thought I heard someone," she says. A furrow appears between her eyebrows. "What was that yesterday?"

My stomach knots at the thought of what I've got to say to my parents. The talk we need to have.

"Is Dad asleep?"

"I think so." Suddenly she pales. "Has something happened to you?"

"No, no. I'm just sad."

"What are you sad about?"

"I just want to be happy."

"Well, yes, of course you're allowed to want that." She looks confused.

"Am I?"

"Yes. All of us should be happy."

"But none of us actually are," I say.

"Astrid..." She reaches for my hand and gives it a squeeze. "I know things are tough right now with Cecilie. But we're doing everything we can to get her better. Your sister is bound to—"

"Good morning!" My dad enters the kitchen in pyjamas. He yawns, scratching his belly.

I start to cry. I don't even realize until Mum is suddenly holding me.

"It'll be fine," she says, her mouth against my damp cheek. "Cecilie will get better, you'll see."

The TV has been switched on. The sound of the news blares through the kitchen.

"Thomas." Mum turns towards him, her arms still round me.

"Yes, sorry, but I need to think about something other than problems for just two minutes," he says, sinking into a kitchen chair. "Is there coffee?"

Right at that very moment, it happens: something inside me has had enough. I walk up and rip the remote control from his hand, switching the TV off with a click. Dad stares at me as though he's genuinely shocked that someone might switch off a TV he's turned on.

I say, "*Why* don't you want to hear what I'm talking to Mum about?"

"Astrid..." He gives a deep sigh.

The sigh upturns everything inside me.

"Can't you even be bothered to listen to me? Now that I've got something to say for once?!"

He pinches his lips, staring at me.

"I feel like we're… I feel like the four of us are…"

Mum tries to hug me again.

I wriggle out of her grasp. "You've got to hear what I'm saying too, Mum."

She sits down on a chair, exchanging a look with my dad.

"We can't make Cecilie healthy," I say. "We just can't. And I think we should stop trying so hard all the time. She needs to do something herself. With somebody who isn't us. So maybe this psychiatrist is a good thing. And the medication."

The kitchen clock is ticking loudly. Neither of them says a word. I'm on the verge of losing my nerve but then I take a deep breath and continue. "But maybe there is something we can do to make this situation better for all of us. Maybe we can go to family therapy."

It's something I was thinking about last night. Whether we could do what Jonas said they did after his father's death, when they didn't know how to be a family any more.

Dad clears his throat. "Yeah…" he says, massaging his chin so the stubble crackles. "Perhaps a team effort does make sense."

"You think so?" I look at him. "Because sometimes I feel like you can't be bothered with us. Any of us."

"Of course I can be bothered with you. But I'm also responsible for an entire company, Astrid. I can't always drop everything just because there's a crisis at home. Especially when there are crises all the time."

"But that's your duty," I say. "To find the time and energy to deal with us. Even when we're totally mental, and you don't understand the first fucking thing about it."

There's an awkward moment. As though I've said something that you can't say aloud in our family.

"You're right," he says at last.

Mum still hasn't said anything. She's just sitting rigidly in her chair.

"OK, well, we'll have to figure something out then." Dad clears his throat again. "I suppose we should take a look at our options for … some sort of counselling." He glances sidelong at Mum.

"It just feels an admission of failure." When she finally speaks, her voice is shaking. "Like we don't know how to be a family any more."

I still think it should be my dad giving Mum a hug. But it's me going up and putting my arms round her.

Dad drives off at ten past eight. Mum drives off at twenty to nine. She asks if I'm OK being alone with Cecilie. I don't really know what the alternative would be because Mum will probably be fired if she keeps asking for more days working from home.

"It's fine," I say. "Don't worry about it."

She looks like she can't think about anything else. "I'll be home at half past three. Thanks for talking to us." She gives my arm a squeeze. "I think you're awesome."

"Do you think Dad feels the same?" I blurt out a small, clumsy laugh.

"Yes," she says. "We've always thought we made the two most awesome girls in the world."

As soon as Mum has gone, I text Jonas. I say I'm sorry I forgot the anniversary of his father's death, and that I'd love to go with him to the churchyard one day and offer up a bucket hat if he wants. It sounds like he's happy about it but of course I can't be sure he's not just pretending. So I try to come up with something about how sorry I am if I've been mean about Veronica and that it's only because really I want him all to myself. But no matter what words I use I sound like an idiot, so in the end I delete the whole message and hope he can just read between the lines, that he'll understand it's not exactly easy admitting when you're jealous.

My sister sleeps in till half past ten. I look in on her several times. She's lying on her side, her mouth open, the occasional smack of her lips.

Then, as I'm watching her, she wakes up.

"Creepy! What are you doing?!"

"I want to talk to you about something."

She sits up, wide-eyed. Evidently, she's remembering that less than twenty-four hours ago she spat out a doomsday prophecy about my future love life and threw a hairbrush at the back of my head.

"Oh no. Don't be angry with me!" She slips back down on to the bed and puts her hands over her ears. "I said I was sorry!"

I stand there for a while, watching her hide. I think I understand how she's feeling. I think I know how much it hurts when someone is growing into a whole person before your eyes and you're not growing anywhere.

"We can talk about it later," I say.

"Can we?" She peeps out.

"It's nothing bad. But sure." I shrug.

"Shall we watch something?"

"Why don't we listen to an audiobook instead?"

"About what?" She wrinkles her nose.

"Something about thinking positive. I need that."

After dinner and two hours of TV on the sofa, I go into the garden. Making for the old swings, I wedge my bum into one of the narrow orange plastic seats. Then I rock slowly back and forth, composing the text to Kristoffer that I have no idea how to write.

Hey ... yesterday got kind of stupid. Do you have a hangover today?

He answers instantly, as though he's been waiting for my message.

Hey. Yeah, the whole thing was pretty stupid. And yes, I have an improbably hideous hangover today.

I wish he'd text something else, something more. I wish he'd reach out, ask me something. But although I wait no more words come.

Are you ready for tomorrow? is the only thing I can think of to write.

This time he doesn't answer for ages. Not until twenty minutes later does the message pop up:

Yup. Ready as anyone can be.

And that's that.

Not long after, my sister comes out and sits on the swing beside me.

"Nice sunset," she says.

I sense a tiny prickle of optimism in my chest at her mention of the sky.

"What was it you wanted to talk about earlier?"

We swing for a bit before I answer. "I told Mum and Dad I'm sick of our situation. Not just you. All of us."

"Because of me."

"No."

"Yes, it's because of me." She's staring straight ahead.

There's not really any point in lying.

"OK, but … now we've got to try and help each other make things better again. All four of us. As a team. As … a family. It's not just you that needs to work on getting better. It's us."

"You mean group therapy?" She wrinkles her nose.

"No, not group therapy, or … well, I don't know. But something where we can figure out how to tackle things together. And I wouldn't be surprised if you're afraid it'll be total bullshit that doesn't work. I'm afraid of that too. But I'd rather hope than be afraid."

"So would I," she says. "If I had a real choice. But I just don't."

We rock languidly back and forth. The sky is changing from a chilly blue to warm orange. The colours melt together infinitely slowly.

"You won't feel like this all your life," I say. "In a year everything will be different. I just know it."

"How can you know that?" she asks.

"Because everything's changing all the time."

Something about getting up the next day feels different. Even the movements: folding my legs over the edge of the bed, walking barefoot into the bathroom, washing my face, bathing my body. I don't think. I just study the grey tones on the tiles, the reflection fogging up in the mirror, my fingers drawing lines.

As I step out of the bathroom, Cecilie goes inside to pee.

Her duvet is still warm when I crawl underneath it.

"What are you doing?" she asks when she comes back in, standing in front of the bed in her pyjamas and yawning.

"Come in here," I say.

She shoots me a look before sitting down on the very edge of the bed. Then I lift the duvet and make space for her.

"I thought you didn't like snuggling with me any more," she says.

"I love snuggling with you!"

She lies down next to me. We're not lying as naturally as usual, and as we stare up at the ceiling, I think we both sense it: the new state of affairs.

"I'm going to school to decorate the trucks," I say. "Want to come? You can go and watch the graduation ceremony. Caroline will be there too."

"I can't," she says.

I want to tell her this is her only chance to see her classmates graduate, her only chance to see Caroline graduate, even though I don't think much of Caroline. I want her to find the courage to show up, even though it's hard and it hurts and it reminds her of what she hasn't got.

Because maybe it would also remind her of everything she could get.

But then I feel her beside me, sense her rapid breathing, the unquiet wave that she is. My sister fights something every day that's invisible but just as hard and real to her as cement. I know I can't push it alone. I can't be the one to save my sister.

"OK," I say.

We lie there silently for a while.

"I'd be happy for you, you know," she says. "If you were dating Kristoffer." She adds with a grimace, "Mum told me to say that."

I can't help laughing. "OK, thanks, but it's not going to happen. We had an argument."

"Like we did?"

"Kind of. But sisters are forever. I know you love me, even though you threw a hairbrush at me. It's not like that with other people," I say.

"Relationships are bullshit, seriously," she says. "Have you guys talked about it?"

"Only texted. About nothing. Doesn't seem like he could care less. Ice-cold. I think he's stopped thinking about me. So … there's not much to be done."

"No," she says.

I elbow her. "No? Is that all you have to say?"

"Hey, you said it yourself."

"Then contradict me! Challenge my world view!"

"Me?"

She pulls a face, but I just wait. And wait. Then slowly she begins to draw a circle in the air with her finger, before turning her head, looking at me and letting her finger land on the tip of my nose.

"Nothing happens until something moves."

"Great," I say. "You're quoting a poster. Genuine wisdom! Love it."

"The theory of relativity," she says, removing her finger. "Albert Einstein. But close, Shrimp."

I burst out laughing.

She stares up at the wall. "And, if you're still not sure, Winnie-the-Pooh would like to tell you that you're braver than you believe, stronger than you seem and smarter than you know. So there you go. Pick one. Einstein or Pooh Bear?"

My feet make the pedals turn swiftly. The morning sun is already strong, and the rays warm the fabric of my clothes.

Veronica and Jonas are in the car park when I arrive, slurping coffee from their neon Thermoses. I stop in front of them, staring at all the trucks ready to be decorated by the first and second years milling around with beech branches and balloons and fluttering banners in their arms.

"Wow," I say.

"Speaking of wow..."

Veronica holds her glasses in place with her index finger while her gaze sweeps me up and down. I've put on a summer dress and borrowed Mum's high-heeled sandals.

"Can we please not talk about that?"

"Sure." She laughs.

"You didn't need to do that on my account." Jonas offers me a sip from his Thermos and I swill down a gulp of tepid coffee. "Or for anyone else's," he adds.

I say, "Shall we get going?"

We tie the light green beech branches firmly to the poles on the open truck beds. A couple of DJs have already turned up and started setting up mixing desks on some of the vehicles, firing off a few beats.

Veronica and I help to clip in place the white banner that the third years gave us two weeks ago.

1 HONK – THAT'S GOOD!
2 HONKS – THAT'S GREAT!
3 HONKS – THAT'S SHOTS!

When we're halfway through decorating the truck, we sit down on the grass and share out the chocolate milk and poppy-seed twists. I'm so nervous all I can do is sit there picking off all the black poppy seeds, until I attract an army of ants and our class has to relocate a few metres away.

Then the cars start rolling into the car park.

We sit watching all the cap-wearing red-and-white graduates as they throng past us with their parents, siblings and grandparents. Some of them smile at us, but most look fairly serious. They're excited, of course, about the principal's and the student council president's speeches, about the diploma presentations – those few tottering seconds when they receive applause and a handshake onstage. But they're probably most excited about the truck ride. The conclusion of three of the most important years of their lives.

I feel a twinge in my chest with each family that goes past.

A twinge for every proud set of parents beside their son or daughter.

It could have been my parents. It could have been Cecilie

walking past in a white dress, beaming, about to move on with her life.

Jonas hugs me from behind, wedging his chin between my shoulder and my face.

"It'll be Cecilie next year," he says.

"I hope so."

"It will be," he says. Then he whispers, "Hell, and in two years it'll be us!"

Once we've finished decorating, there's nothing left to do but wait. The bass thuds rhythmically from the trucks. More and more people are beginning to show up – people from the town who've just come to enjoy the sight of the happy graduates being sent off.

All these strange faces make me feel like I'm drowning in the crowd. We're together for a purpose but I'm also completely alone.

Then the parents start trickling outside. They're red-cheeked and smiling, gathering round the trucks, readying phones and cameras.

I look for Kristoffer's mum and granddad but I can't see them anywhere. Finally, over where the first years are decorating the third-year student trucks, the protagonists themselves stream out of the main doors. It feels like a wave of white birds approaching in a single flock. I almost forget to inhale. I can feel my breath way up in my throat.

Then I see him. He's turned his cap slightly so that the shadow doesn't fall straight across his brow. His black hair is poking out. His eyes are flitting everywhere; he's being patted and clapped on the back by people around him; he lifts his cap and says hello. And he's smiling all the while, smiling so much I almost feel the urge to sob at the thought that none of those smiles are meant for me.

There are several rows of people ahead of me and although I try to barge my way forward, the clump of bodies is virtually still and I don't get there in time: suddenly I see him on the truck bed with the others. He's already got a beer in his hand.

The music on the trucks is pumping now, and I try a few clumsy hops up and down, shouting his name as loudly as I can: "*Kristoffer! Kristoffer!*"

He doesn't hear me.

I'm completely invisible.

Then I remember something, a last-ditch attempt to make myself visible. Digging my hand into my bag, I grab the whistle I tore off his neck what feels like a very long time ago. The mouthpiece is cold and hard between my lips, and I take a single deep breath before I blow with all my strength.

An elderly man right in front of me claps a hand to his ear, saying exasperatedly, "Do you mind!?"

But I blow again. This time even louder.

More people turn round. And at last they start to hear me up on the truck bed too. At last Kristoffer turns his gaze down towards the sea of people. Towards me.

We make eye contact.

I've still got the whistle between my lips but now it slips out of my mouth, landing somewhere on the tarmac underneath my feet.

He looks at me.

I look at him.

It feels like eternity passes right there.

Then he jostles his way through the others on the truck, barging people aside, walks down the ramp and takes the final stretch in a single bound. I'm still standing on my patch of tarmac, rooted, until he stops in front of me. We're pushed together in the crush, half a metre between us at most.

"Hi," he says.

"Hi." My mouth is dry. I run my tongue around the inside of it a few times before I find more words. "I just wanted to say congratulations on everything."

"Thanks." Someone calls his name and he glances quickly, almost impatiently, over his shoulder.

For a moment, I consider scurrying away across the road like a mouse, vanishing into the throng and dropping all thought of ever seeing him again. But then he turns his eyes back to me and I take a deep breath.

"I'd also like to say sorry."

"For what?" His face looks abruptly empty, as though

he's rinsed it clean of all emotion.

"For … you know."

"No."

The blood rushes to my cheeks. "I'm sorry for the things I said. I didn't mean them. I didn't mean you don't make me happy. You do."

"I know that," he says.

"Um, OK."

"Stop looking so shocked. I told you: you're like an open book."

"You don't think I'm a total idiot because of that night?"

"Yeah, I do," he says. "Now you come to ask. But I probably wasn't the best version of myself either."

His classmates on the truck start clapping and calling his name in a steady rhythm.

"*Stoooo-ffer!*" Clap-clap-clap.

"*Stoooo-ffer!*" Clap-clap-clap.

Glancing across the car park, I can see all the trucks are full, tailboards shut and ready to leave. They're only waiting for Kristoffer.

"We can talk tomorrow," he says. "When I've woken up?"

I nod.

He starts walking backwards. "And hey, I'm glad you apologized, OK?" He smiles, finally he smiles. And before I can think twice I grab his arms and pull him back to me. Our front teeth clash, my mouth is way too dry, he's laughing through it all, and still the kiss is perfect.

And over much too fast.

We let go, and he says, "See you," before making his way back.

People step aside to let him pass. The ramp up to the truck has already been removed but he takes his classmates' outstretched hands, and they heave him up. Seconds later, the driver honks before starting the engine with a roar.

Kristoffer finds a place at the end of the truck where I can see him. There he stays.

The first trucks start driving off to the sound of loud beeps and thudding bass. People follow, the whole crowd moving across the car park like a swiftly rolling wave.

Jonas and Veronica break out of the wave, come towards me and put their arms round me from either side.

I'm clamped in a friendly vice.

"So long," says Jonas. "Bye-bye, baby!"

Kristoffer lifts his hand and waves. His is the last truck to trundle away.

I wave back. It's hard to tear myself from the sight of him as he gets smaller and smaller.

There's a pressure in my chest when I think of all our futures. It squashes and stabs. But right now, in this exact moment, I feel like things are OK the way they are. And these are probably the moments I should start focusing on.

The trucks have disappeared over the horizon. People begin to drift away.

"Shall we go for a swim?" asks Veronica. "Or do you want to go into town and watch them dance round the fountain? Or we could grab some ice cream?"

"I don't fancy watching anybody dance round a blasphemous baby spraying water out of his green willie," says Jonas. "I vote for ice cream."

"Yeah, ice cream!" Veronica jumps up and down on the spot. "Haven't we earned it?"

"Sure," I say, turning my gaze towards the sky. "I think we've earned it all."

RESOURCES

If you or anyone you know is struggling with their mental health, the resources below may be helpful for getting the help you need.

Mind – mind.org.uk

CALM (Campaign Against Living Miserably) – thecalmzone.net

Samaritans – samaritans.org

PAPYRUS HOPELINEUK – papyrus-uk.org

The Association for Child and Adolescent Mental Health Service – acamh.org

YoungMinds – youngminds.org.uk

Black Minds Matter UK – blackmindsmatteruk.com

Just Ask a Question – jaaq.org

ABOUT THE AUTHOR

Lise Villadsen is the Danish breakout star behind a series of electrifying and critically acclaimed young adult novels centred around complex family dynamics and youth mental health issues. Villadsen began to pen novels at the age of fourteen and made her lauded debut in 2018. She lives in Copenhagen.

The award-winning *In Your Orbit* is her first novel translated into English.

ABOUT THE TRANSLATOR

Caroline Waight is an award-winning literary translator working from Danish, German and Norwegian.

She has translated a wide range of fiction and non-fiction, with recent publications including *The Lobster's Shell* by Caroline Albertine Minor (Granta, 2022), *Island* by Siri Ranva Hjelm Jacobsen (Pushkin Press, 2021) and *The Chief Witness* by Sayragul Sauytbay and Alexandra Cavelius (Scribe, 2021). She lives and works near London.